# Polar Day

By Julie Flanders

Ink Smith Publishing
www.ink-smith.com

Polar Day
By Julie Flanders

ISBN: 978-1-939156-63-1

Ink Smith Publishing
P.O. Box Box 1086
Glendora CA
www.inksmith.com

# Table of Contents

# Chapter 1
## Fairbanks, Alaska
*May 23, 2013*

Max Fugate jogged down Wendell Avenue and took a right into Griffin Park, passing under the moose antler arch at the entrance. He made a quick right again and increased his speed as he ran along the park's paved jogging trail. A light breeze played through his thinning black hair, and he could hear the "kaanc kanc" calls of the Mallard ducks that came to Fairbanks every spring and stayed throughout the summer. He could hardly blame them. Even now, when Fairbanks was experiencing a record-breaking heat wave, the likes of which Max had never seen, there was nothing like Alaska in the summer.

Streetlights lined the park trail, but there was no need for them during the summer season. Despite the fact that he had lived in Alaska all his life, Max never tired of watching the sun just start to set as he enjoyed his late night runs. Knowing that it would rise again in just a few short hours was magical to him. He could never understand why some Alaskans complained about the long summer days. He never wanted them to end. The only complaint he had about the summer was the annual infestation of mosquitoes. But even they weren't bothering him now. He still had a few weeks left to enjoy the peaceful and glorious weather before the winged pests reached their noisy peak in June and July.

He smiled as he passed a pole with a sign advertising next month's Midnight Sun baseball game at Growden Memorial Park. The game had been a summer solstice tradition since the early 1900s, and Max hadn't missed a year since he was thirteen and the flu had forced him to stay home. This year, the Alaska Goldpanners would be taking on the Chugiak Chinooks and the game would begin at its normal time of 10:35 PM. To Max's knowledge, the game had never needed to be postponed or delayed because of darkness. The sun always stuck around until the last out was in the books.

Max hoped he could talk Kris into going to the game with him this year. If they were going to make it as a couple, they had to find some common interests. If Kris didn't like baseball, Max was fairly certain the relationship would come to an end. There was only so much he could let slide.

He slowed to a jog and pricked his ears at an unfamiliar noise behind him. Or was it in front of him? Was it footsteps? It wasn't unusual to find another runner savoring the beautiful May weather in the park. But it didn't sound like footsteps. Max glanced around him but couldn't identify the sound.

He felt an odd sensation and increased his speed back up to a run. While he didn't know what he had heard, he could say with certainty that he didn't like the feeling it gave him. Slowing his pace again, Max turned around and jogged backwards as he looked for the source of the noise. He saw nothing. There was no one behind him but, as he turned back to face the front, he saw a man ahead of him on the trail. Wearing a Seattle Mariners baseball hat over strands of dark brown hair, the man stood still and stared directly at Max. He looked familiar, like someone Max had seen at the hospital.

"Do I know you?" Max asked.

The man vanished without giving an answer.

Max closed his eyes briefly and focused on steadying his breathing. Was he seeing things? When he opened his eyes again, the man was nowhere to be seen. How could a person disappear that quickly? Max shook his head and scoffed at himself, knowing he was being foolish. There hadn't been anyone ahead of him on the trail. The setting sun had obviously played a trick on his eyes. Max forced himself to ignore the question that niggled at him as he continued to run. If he had merely imagined the man in front of him, how, and for that manner why, had he managed to see the Mariners' logo so clearly?

Max came to a startled halt as he ran straight into something that blocked his way on the trail. But there was nothing in front of him. Breathing heavily, he raised his hand out in front of him and felt a solid mass directly in his path. It felt like a man's chest....

"What's going on?" Max said, trying to keep the rising fear out of his voice. "Is this someone's idea of a prank?"

Max looked to his left and right as the skin on the back of his neck stood on end. He saw no one.

"Who's..."

Max couldn't finish his question before an unseen hand gripped his throat and began to squeeze. He gasped for air as he brought his hands to his throat and clawed at nothing. He heard a chuckle as the fingers around his throat tightened and threatened to crush his windpipe.

As suddenly as the invisible terror had grabbed him, it eased the pressure on this throat and pushed him into the grass alongside the trail. Max coughed and gulped in air as he tried to get his bearings. He screamed for help, praying someone was around to hear him.

No one was. And even if they had been, no one could have made it to Max in time.

Before he could stand up, Max felt a prickly sensation on his arms as a wave of intense heat washed over him. At the same time, he heard the voice of a man chanting in a foreign language. His nose twitched as his nostrils picked up the scent of fire. Was something burning in the park? Still clutching his throat, Max glanced around but saw no signs of smoke. The wind rustled through the trees but Max could not feel its cooling breeze. He could feel nothing but heat. And he still heard the strange and unintelligible chanting.

Max struggled to stand but froze in place as he noticed tendrils of smoke rising from his arms. He once again heard the chuckle of his unseen assailant before catching another glimpse of dark hair underneath a Mariners hat.

Max yelled for help and heard his own voice echoing around the empty park. Wisps of smoke emerged from his legs and a spark ignited into flame on his arm. He collapsed back on the ground as something in his brain remembered the fire instructions he had received as a child during fire safety week at school. Stop, drop and roll.

Max rolled in the grass but the flames continued to erupt on his body. He screamed in terror as his legs and feet burst into flames. He brought burning hands to his chest and tried to rip off his burning t-shirt, but the flames merely jumped to his face and head.

## Polar Day

Within seconds, the sounds of the fire had engulfed Max's screams. While his body burned, sparks from the flames leapt into the darkening sky. The fire burned a circle in the grass around Max's body. The last thing Max ever saw was the figure of a dark haired man standing over him, watching him burn.

Five minutes later, the fire collapsed into itself and dissolved into smoldering embers in the parched dirt. Nothing remained of Max Fugate but a charred and grotesque husk of a human body.

\*\*\*\*

# Chapter 2

Jamie closed the door of his apartment behind him and caught his breath as he leaned against it. He struggled to contain his excitement over the successful execution of his plan; of his dream. He had done it. And it was all just the beginning.

He knew he had made the right decision in kicking off his plan on the sacred day of May 23. It had made the whole experience even more exhilarating. That exhilaration hadn't lessened now that he was home, as he could still smell the delicious scent of fire and the aroma of burning flesh in his nostrils. It was more intoxicating than any drug could ever be.

Walking to his bedroom, he took off his Mariners cap and set it on top of his faux wood dresser. He knew that he had not succeeded 100 percent and that his victim had caught glimpses of him prior to his triumph, but what concern was that now? It wasn't as if the man was around to identify him. And he had made certain that no one else was on the jogging trail. No one alive had seen him, he was sure of it.

After his precious flames had burned his victim to little more than a skeleton, Jamie had quickly hidden the charred remains in the brush among the trees that lined the jogging trail, covering the corpse with as many branches and leaves as he could find. He didn't want his first victim discovered just yet. The discovery would have much more impact later in the summer.

He smiled now as he sat down on his bed and kicked off his shoes. His breathing had finally returned to normal and he was able to review the night's events with an objective eye. No, he hadn't been perfect, but that was to be expected. He was still learning and growing stronger. No opening night is without glitches. But he had performed well enough to know his show was going to last quite a while.

Jamie headed towards his bathroom and prepared to take a shower.

He hated to wash the smell of the smoke and flames off of him but it had to be done. He would be at work in just a few short hours for the start of another day.

He glanced out his window and watched the sun finally drop beneath the horizon. It was 11:40 PM and the day had ended. What a glorious day it had been.

****

# Chapter 3
*June 21, 2013*

"Can you stop thinking about work for one minute?" Tessa Washington took a sip of her Coke and pushed her sunglasses up on her nose. "We're here to watch the game," she said.

"How do you know I'm thinking about work?" Danny Fitzpatrick asked.

"Because it's obvious. I asked you if you wanted me to get you a Frito pie at the concession stand and you didn't even respond. Then I noticed Sox was pawing at your leg and you ignored him. I know perfectly well you're going over our case in your head."

Danny glanced down at his dog, a medium-sized black mutt with the face of a spaniel and the body of a poodle. "You need something, Sox?" he asked. The dog responded by thumping his tail on the grass.

"Sox is fine," he said, returning his attention to Tessa. "But God knows I don't want to miss out on the Frito pie."

Danny leaned forward in his lawn chair and grabbed his wallet out of the back pocket of his khaki shorts. He took a ten-dollar bill out and held it up to Tessa, a petite African-American woman with a pile of dark brown braids on her head. Dressed to the nines as always, Tessa managed to look stylish whether she was working, going out on the town or sitting on a lawn chair at a baseball game. Tonight she wore a white sheath dress with matching gladiator sandals and a pair of oversized sunglasses.

"I'll pay since you're sparing me the torture of standing in line over there," Danny said, gesturing to the group of children and adults gathered around the stand. "Will this cover it?"

Tessa nodded and grabbed the bill as she stood up from her chair. "Do you want a beer too?"

Danny shook his head. "No, just a Coke."

# Polar Day

Danny had cut back on his drinking in the past few months, but he couldn't deny there were still plenty of days when all he wanted to do after work was go home and drink himself into a stupor. The responsibility of caring for his dog was often the only thing that stopped him. He reached down and scratched Sox's ears as Tessa walked off towards the stand. "I wasn't ignoring you, buddy. What's up?"

Sox licked his hand and rolled onto his back, offering his stomach for Danny to rub.

"I should have guessed it was a belly rub you wanted. What else?"

The dog wiggled in the grass and continued to thump his tail on the ground as Danny scratched his belly.

"I wonder if they sell any dog treats here," Danny mused. "I should have told Tessa to get you something. Maybe a hot dog."

Danny was a tall and thin man, with large brown eyes and a mop of matching hair that was in a constantly unkempt state regardless of how often he combed it. In the past year he had taken to wearing a perpetual layer of stubble on his pale face, something he had decided gave him a sophisticated air of masculinity. It was also very convenient since he had hated to shave ever since he hit puberty. Danny had a long nose and wore the strain of his job and the grief of his past on his face, giving him a drawn and melancholy expression. He was a loner who preferred the company of his dog to that of most people.

Danny looked around Growden Memorial Park and had to remind himself that it was already 10:15 at night. The sun remained high in the cloudless blue sky as players for the Alaska Goldpanners and the Chugiak Chinooks prepared for the upcoming game. The temperature was a scorching 85 degrees, as Fairbanks was experiencing a record heat wave that showed no signs of letting up with the arrival of the official summer season.

Tessa had talked Danny into coming with her to this year's Midnight Sun Baseball Game, a tradition he had heard about ever since moving to Fairbanks. The first pitch would be thrown out in just about 20 minutes and, according to the experts, the sun would set and rise again before the game was over. The game had never required any artificial lighting, as the twilight provided enough light even during the brief time that the sunset.

Danny had completely ignored everything about the game and the Goldpanners, Fairbanks' semi-professional team, last summer, which had been his first in Alaska. When he'd impulsively moved to Fairbanks from his hometown of Chicago following the murder of his wife, Caroline, Danny had made every effort to ignore anything and everything that could bring him some element of joy. Everything, except alcohol at least.

Baseball had been one of those things he'd ignored. He'd loved the game for as long as he could remember and had been a White Sox fan since childhood. While Caroline had been a Cubs fan, she'd still reluctantly agreed to celebrate the Sox's 2005 World Series win with him, a win he'd never expected he'd see and which could still make him smile.

Fairbanks, and, for that matter, the state of Alaska, didn't have any major league sports to call their own. But residents embraced the Goldpanners, a member of the Western Semi-Pro Baseball Association, and regularly filled the stands of Growden Park to cheer them on during the all-too brief Alaskan summer.

Tessa Washington was his closest friend in Fairbanks and now also his partner since he'd left cold cases behind and joined her in homicide following the retirement of her former partner the previous month. Danny had spent most of his adult life as a homicide detective in Chicago but after Caroline's death he swore he'd never work homicide again. He'd changed his mind after growing weary of sifting through cold cases, the majority of which he knew would never be solved and when he had the chance to partner with Tessa. He respected her as a cop as much as he liked her as a person.

Tessa was a baseball fanatic like him and her enthusiasm for the Goldpanners had gradually worn off on Danny. They'd never replace the White Sox for him, but they were fun to watch and provided a great way to enjoy the long summer days and the warm weather that never lasted long enough in Alaska. As long as he remembered to use enough DEET to keep the mosquitoes at bay. Danny had dealt with plenty of mosquitoes in Chicago but he'd never seen anything like the swarms of insects that invaded Fairbanks every summer. He'd been told that Alaska's mosquitoes were legendary and it wasn't hard to understand why.

Polar Day

But while he'd grudgingly become a fan of the Goldpanners and even bought an official team t-shirt sporting their customary red and gold colors, he still remembered his beloved White Sox every time he called his dog by name. When he'd adopted the dog from the local animal shelter back in April, he'd known immediately what he'd wanted to call him. While he'd briefly considered Comiskey, after the legendary park where the White Sox had played for most of his life, both Tessa and his on-again, off-again girlfriend Amanda had convinced him of the foolishness of that choice. It hadn't taken much convincing, and he'd named Sox before he and the dog had returned home to Danny's apartment after leaving the shelter.

As Sox jumped up to attend to an itch on his paw by biting it with a ferocity that made Danny cringe, Danny glanced around for Tessa. He smiled as he saw her heading towards their chairs along the right field fence just in time for the playing of the National Anthem.

"Lord that line was something else," Tessa said as she handed Danny his Coke and Frito pie. "You're going up there next time if we decide to get anything else."

"I'll make sure to make my pie last then," Danny said. "I don't want any part of all those screaming kids. Especially not in this heat." He shuddered as he took another look back at the line, which had only continued to grow.

Danny took a bite of his pie and set his Coke on the ground before he and Tessa stood up for the National Anthem. He knew better than to set his pie down, as Sox would down it before the first line of the song was complete.

The park erupted in cheers as the anthem completed and the umpire yelled out the customary, "Play ball!" Danny and Tessa settled back into their chairs and returned to eating their Frito pies.

"Too bad Maya didn't come with us," Danny said. "Sox would like the company."

Maya was Tessa's Siberian Husky and Sox's best canine friend. The two dogs had immediately bonded after Danny adopted Sox and the group regularly walked together at Griffin Park.

"I told you, she hates the crowds," Tessa said between bites of her pie. "When I brought her last year I had to leave before the third inning. And she'd never make it in this heat. She hates heat as much as you

10

do."

"I don't hate heat."

"You've whined about the heat wave every day this month."

"Well it is odd, isn't it? Having temperatures this high in Fairbanks?"

"It is. But I haven't heard anyone else complaining. Come to think of it, I seem to remember you complaining non-stop about the cold during the winter too."

Danny ignored his partner and finished off his pie in spite of his plan to make it last throughout the game. He wiped his mouth with a napkin and rolled up the wrapper and napkin into a ball in his lap, which immediately fell to the ground when he and Tessa and everyone else in the park stood up to cheer the Goldpanners' first home run of the game.

Before sitting back down Danny picked up the garbage and strolled over to the nearest garbage can, causing Sox to bark and pull on his leash, which was attached to Danny's chair.

He laughed and scratched the dog's ears as he returned to his seat. "I was gone two seconds, buddy," he said.

Danny tried to focus on the game in front of him, cheering once again as the Goldpanners hit another home run and took a 2-0 lead, but he found his mind wandering. Tessa was right when she said he was distracted. But not by the murder-suicide they had investigated that morning, which was as close to an open-and-shut case as any cop could expect to receive. He hadn't been thinking about that at all. Instead, he had been thinking about the thing that had occupied his mind for months now. Aleksei Nechayev.

And make no mistake; he knew without a doubt that the Nechayev who remained at large and was wanted for numerous homicides was a thing and not a person. The Russian-born vampire who had nearly killed him back in December never left Danny's thoughts for long.

It wasn't just the vampire himself who had managed to take up residence in Danny's psyche. It was the very idea that he existed. Danny had refused to believe in that possibility when Amanda, a near victim of Nechayev, had confided in him about her theories. But he'd been forced to admit she was right when he'd come face to face with Aleksei's fangs and monstrous persona himself.

11

Polar Day

Now, he was sure he saw vampires on every corner. He wondered how many others were out there and felt immense relief to be in the season of near constant daylight in Alaska. He glanced up at the sun, grateful that no vampires could possibly be on hand at tonight's game.

Danny dreaded the return of winter and the darkness that Aleksei had taught him was a vampire's best friend. But it wasn't only the vampires who played with Danny's fears. Now that he knew they existed, he knew there was a good chance that other supposedly mythological creatures existed as well. Every howling dog became a werewolf in Danny's mind. Every creak in his apartment was a ghost.

In the six months since Danny had been rescued from certain death in Aleksei's haunted asylum he had spent most of his time combing through old case files to look for unexplained events that could point to supernatural causes. Even when he had left cold cases behind for his current position in homicide he had haunted the office during the nights and weekends and searched through endless case files for signs of the paranormal.

He had found plenty to arouse his suspicions, but had nowhere to take his concerns. Not ready to become the Fox Mulder of the Fairbanks police department, Danny had not shared his late night detective work with anyone except Amanda. He already knew that no one else would believe him. Worse, he knew that divulging his new-found convictions would likely lead to a stint in a psychiatric facility.

The raucous sounds of cheering around him interrupted Danny's thoughts. He glanced around to see that he was the only person who remained seated. The Goldpanners' first baseman had hit a grand slam and the fans were ecstatic as the players ran around the bases. Danny stood up and joined in the cheering, which caused Sox to bark excitedly and jump at his waist.

Tessa gave him a sideways glance. "About time you joined us. Can you even try to pay attention to the game?"

"We're cheering, aren't we?" Danny let out a whoop, picked up Sox, and patted the dog's paws together to simulate claps.

Tessa rolled her eyes as the cheers subsided and the two returned to their seats. Sox hopped down from Danny's lap and returned to sniffing the grass around their chairs.

"I know you love baseball," she said. "I thought this game would

12

finally help you stop obsessing about our cases."

"I wasn't obsessing about our cases," Danny said truthfully. "I was obsessing about other things. But I'm back in the moment now and ready to cheer on our Goldpanners to victory. So why don't we both just focus on the game?"

Tessa happily agreed and the two cheered as the Goldpanners notched another home run and then groaned as the Chinooks drove in some runs of their own and tightened up the score. As the game progressed and the clock struck midnight, the fans all stood up from their seats in the bleachers or their chairs along the lawn.

"What's going on?" Danny asked.

"It's midnight. That means it's time to sing 'Alaska's Flag'."

Tessa laughed at the clueless look on Danny's face. "It's the state song," she said as she started to sing.

Eight stars of gold on a field of blue,

Alaska's flag, may it mean to you...

Danny had never heard the song in his life and didn't know a single word of it, but he stood up gamely and tried to pretend he was following along. Sox stood alert with his ears cocked and let out a howl in an attempt to join the singing.

The song came to a rousing conclusion and everyone applauded before returning to their seats for the resumption of the game. Danny watched as a teenage boy and girl walked hand in hand towards the large group of trees that lined the outfield. It didn't take any detective work to figure out what they had planned. He smiled as he thought of his own teenage years and his numerous trips to Comiskey every summer. While he had brought plenty of girls to baseball games, he'd never considered leaving the game to screw around with any of them. When he was at Comiskey, he was there to watch the White Sox. And if the girl he was with didn't like that, he knew he wouldn't be spending much more time with her.

The teenagers disappeared and Danny's attention turned to a gray-haired male jogger who was circling the field on the Growden Park running track. Danny felt a flutter of jealousy as he watched the man run. He was obviously athletic and fit; something Danny had once been before he had decided to drown the pain out of his life with alcohol and cigarettes. Now he doubted he could run even half the length of the track without wheezing and gasping for air. He needed to do something to start getting back in shape.

Danny's jealousy turned to surprise when the jogger stopped suddenly on the track. Danny caught a glimpse of something in front of the man, what looked to be a shadow of a figure, but whatever it was immediately disappeared. Perhaps it had just been a trick of the light from the soon to be setting sun. But it looked to Danny as if the man had run into something. The man tried to start running again, only to again appear to run right into something in front of him. This time, Danny could see nothing there. He nudged Tessa.

"What do you think is wrong with that guy?" he asked, pointing towards the jogger.

Before Tessa could respond, the man suddenly grabbed at this throat. He stumbled backwards, clearly struggling to maintain his balance.

"I think he's choking," Tessa said. "We need to get over there and help him."

Both Danny and Tessa quickly stood up but the man tumbled to the grass next to the track before either of them could move. To their horror, orange flames began to crawl up the man's arms and legs. His anguished screams permeated the park, causing even the baseball players to stop their play and turn towards the sound.

Danny and Tessa sprinted towards the man, with Danny calling 911 and reporting a person on fire as they did. Before they even reached the burning man they could hear the sirens of the Fairbanks fire trucks making their way towards the park.

The man was completely engulfed in fire by the time Danny and Tessa arrived at the track, and the flames had turned from orange to a scorching yellow color with shards of white. It crossed Danny's mind that somewhere he had learned that white flames were the hottest. Another scream of agony from the man pushed the idea from Danny's mind.

Tessa leaned forward and tossed the beach blanket she had grabbed from her chair onto the man's body in an attempt to smother the fire. The blanket had little to no effect as it was immediately swallowed up in the flames. She jumped backwards and fell into Danny as the heat of the fire singed the hair on her arms.

"Are you okay?" he yelled.

"I'm fine," Tessa answered, holding a hand to her face to shield it. "I didn't get burned."

The concession stand workers came up behind Danny and Tessa, moving their way through the crowd of spectators who had gathered and now stared at the burning man in horror.

"We've got a fire extinguisher," the woman in charge of the concession stand yelled as she ran up behind the two detectives.

Danny grabbed the extinguisher and sprayed the foam solution onto the flames. The solution barely made a dent before it was swallowed up as quickly as Tessa's blanket.

"What the hell is going on?" Danny yelled.

The heat from the flames became unbearable and all of the would-be rescuers were forced to step back. Sox barked and yelped as the fire continued to burn and the flames shot higher towards the sky.

To everyone's relief, fire engines pulled onto the grounds and firefighters spilled towards the dying man.

"Clear the area, folks," the fire chief yelled.

The group complied and stood transfixed as the firefighters extinguished the flames. The man had long since stopped screaming, and his body no longer writhed in agony on the grass. Danny felt certain he was already dead. Danny glanced down at Sox, who had continued to bark and whimper. He picked the dog up into his arms, shushing him and scratching his ears to keep him quiet.

While no one spoke, all watched in horror as the firefighters' hoses snuffed out the flames, leaving a charred, blackened figure where the jogger had once been.

The fire chief stepped forward and took charge of the crowd. "Folks, we're going to need all of you to stay here. The arson investigators and the police are on their way and we'll need to talk with all of you to see if we can figure out what happened here." He scanned the crowd, stopping when he saw Tessa.

"Detective Washington?" he said.

Tessa managed a feeble smile and stepped forward. "Sure is, Chief. It's been a long time."

"I'm glad to see you here," the chief said. "I have a feeling our team may be requiring your assistance."

Tessa motioned towards Danny. "This is my partner, Detective Fitzpatrick. You've got two homicide detectives at your service."

The chief shook Danny's offered hand and patted Sox's nose. "Fitzpatrick, huh? I don't think we've met."

"I haven't lived in Fairbanks long," Danny said. "I'm sure we haven't."

The arrival of police cars and the arson investigation team interrupted the conversation.

"Listen chief, Tessa and I are in for the duration on this. But as you can see I've got a friend with me," Danny said, gesturing with his free hand toward Sox. "I need to take him home before I can work this." He turned to Tessa. "Do you mind getting started without me?"

"Not at all." She reached out and nuzzled Sox. "Will you stop and feed Maya before you come back? I wasn't planning to be here all night."

"Sure. I'll put a call in to the captain on my way home too. He's probably already been alerted but I'll let him know we were right here the whole time."

Danny put Sox back on the ground and hastily walked to his car. If he hadn't known it, he never would have guessed that a baseball game and a cherished annual tradition had been going on barely thirty minutes earlier. The stench of burning flesh and the horror of the fiery death had chased all sense of frivolity and celebration from the park.

As he got to his car and opened the back door for Sox to hop inside, he glanced back at the crowd milling around the now dead man. He thought again of the shadowy figure he had seen prior to the start of the fire. He no longer thought it had been the setting sun playing tricks on his eyes. He knew someone had been in the jogger's path right before he died.

The identity of that someone, or something, wasn't the only question Danny had as he drove away from the scene of the carnage. How could a man just burst into flames? And Danny had seen the man rolling in the grass in an attempt to smother the fire before it engulfed him. If anything, the movement had only caused the flames to intensify. How could fire become so hot and so intense so quickly?

****

16

# Chapter 4

"What do we have so far?" Danny asked Tessa.

He had returned to the scene of the fire after dropping Sox off at home and checking in on her dog Maya as promised.

"Not much. Rizzo's here now," Tessa said, pointing towards a paunchy, pale man who was leaning over the still smoldering remains of the jogger.

Anthony Rizzo was the chief arson investigator in the Fairbanks police department and, as he had told everyone in the department more times than anyone could count, he was retiring in September. Danny could imagine how much he hated to have a case like this thrown at him when he only had a few months left on the job.

Danny wandered over to Rizzo and the fire chief, who were now talking to Danny's boss, Captain Jack Meyer. The three turned and nodded a greeting to him as he approached.

"You want me to start canvassing?" Danny asked. "Have you started checking cell phones yet?"

"Tessa told us you two saw this poor devil before the fire started," Meyer said, ignoring Danny's questions.

"Yeah, I did. He was running along and it crossed my mind that I was jealous of how in shape he seemed. No sense at all that there was anything wrong with him. Next thing I know he stopped and I thought I saw something in front of him, like a shadow or something. I thought it was just a trick of the light. Then he grabbed his throat and stumbled like he couldn't keep his balance. Tessa and I thought he was choking so we got up to run over and help him. You know what happened then."

"Tessa didn't mention seeing anything in front of the guy," Meyer said.

"She didn't. She wasn't even looking in his direction until I pointed him out to her after I noticed he had stopped. I wouldn't have seen him either if I hadn't noticed two kids heading into the woods right before this happened."

Meyer pointed at two frightened teenagers standing huddled together near the outfield fence. "Those two?" he asked.

"Yeah."

"From what we know they were the closest to the scene. Why don't you go talk to them? We still need their statements."

Danny walked over to the boy and girl he had watched walking into the woods earlier in the evening; before the baseball game had turned into a waking nightmare of fire and death. He noticed the kids covering their faces in futile attempts to block the still permeating smell of burning flesh.

"You two all right?" he asked.

The boy, who was dark-haired, thin and lanky, looked as if his torso had not caught up with a recent growth spurt, spoke first.

"We're fine," he said, clutching the girl's hand protectively. The two of them looked no more than 15 years old.

The girl, her red hair pulled back into a ponytail, was as petite as the boy was tall.

"We didn't see anything," she said.

Danny made note of her defensiveness. "What were you doing in the woods?" he asked, already knowing the answer.

"Nothing," the girl replied.

"That's not an answer," Danny said. "You were obviously doing something."

"We were just taking a walk, okay?" the girl said.

Danny held his hands up, palms facing the teens. "How about you just tell me your names? I think we got off on the wrong foot here and I'm not sure why."

"I'm Will and she's Melissa," the boy said, still holding his girlfriend's hand in what looked to Danny like a death grip.

"Okay Will and Melissa. I'm Detective Fitzpatrick. And I was sitting right over there," Danny said, pointing to his and Tessa's now abandoned lawn chairs, "when I saw you two go off into these woods right before the fire started."

"So?" the boy asked.

"So it might seem a little weird, you two leaving the game and disappearing into the woods right before all hell breaks loose. It's especially weird since you say you were doing 'nothing.'"

The two teens glanced at each other and remained silent.

"Are you afraid to tell me you were going in there to have sex? You think I give a shit about that?"

"We don't want to get in trouble," Melissa said. "If our parents…"

"I'm not saying a word to your parents or anyone else. And trust me, there isn't a soul here who wouldn't have known what you two were up to when they saw you sneaking off into these woods."

The teens looked at the ground.

"Just walk me through it," Danny said. "You may have seen or heard something and didn't even realize it."

Melissa let out a breath. "Alright. Right after we walked past those trees, we heard the jogger make a weird noise. We turned around and thought we saw something in front of him."

"What was it?"

Will answered. "We didn't know. It was like a shadow or something. It was weird."

Melissa nodded in agreement.

Danny kept his face impassive. "What then?"

"Nothing," Melissa said. "It was there and then it wasn't. Next thing we knew the guy started burning."

Will turned red and stared at the ground.

"What else?" Danny asked. "I get the feeling you're leaving something out."

"It was just so crazy," Will said. "We heard someone chanting right before the fire started."

"Chanting? Chanting what?"

"We didn't know. Whatever he was saying, it wasn't in English."

"You said he. So it was definitely a man's voice that you heard?"

"Yes," Melissa answered. "It just sounded like random words from God knows what language. We couldn't tell."

"Does either of you two know any languages besides English?"

"I take Spanish in school," Will said.

"I know some French."

"So you don't think it was either one of those two languages you heard?"

Both teens shook their heads no.

"Not even close to either of them," Will said. "The words sounded kind of harsh."

"We couldn't figure out who was talking," Melissa said. "It was like the voice was right in front of us over by the jogger but we couldn't see anyone."

"We just kind of froze," Will said, hanging his head. "We were so scared."

Danny patted the boy on the shoulder. "So was I, buddy. Everyone here was." He paused before resuming his questions. "When you first went into the woods, did you hear anything else weird before the chanting started? Smell anything?"

Both teens shook their heads. "It was just all the baseball game stuff," Will said.

The conversation was interrupted by a woman calling Will's name as she ran towards the trio. "Will! Will, are you okay?"

"Your mother, I assume?" Danny asked.

The boy nodded.

"You two go catch up to her," Danny said. He fished out a business card from his pocket and handed it to the girl. "Keep this and let me know if you remember anything else that might help us. Thanks for talking with me."

The teens ran as quickly as possible across the field to Will's mother. Danny watched them go before turning to scan the crowd around him. There was an older black couple leaning against the fence and trying to quiet their dog, a nondescript brown mutt who reminded him of Sox. A younger dark-haired white man in a Mariners baseball cap stared at the medical examiners and the coroner as they arrived on the scene. Two middle-aged white women sat on the grass and wiped tears from their eyes.

There were literally thousands of witnesses to this scene of carnage and all of them had to be interviewed. In addition, odds were good that at least 95 percent of the people here had cell phones with them. There was a good chance that someone recorded the fire and may have even caught footage of the jogger before he was burned alive. In spite of the fact that every available officer on the Fairbanks force had been dispatched to the scene it was still going to be a very long night.

Julie Flanders

\*\*\*\*

# Chapter 5

*Danny stumbled through the woods, his dimming flashlight a solitary shard of light in the ink black darkness of the night. His feet felt as if they weighed 100 pounds each as he struggled to lift them enough to walk through the knee-deep snow. He wasn't dressed for winter and his thin shoes had long ago become encased in ice.*

*The wind shrieked through the trees around him, but it couldn't block out the sounds of the footsteps Danny heard coming towards him. Or perhaps footsteps weren't the right word for the sounds he heard. It sounded more like someone was gliding towards him, skiing over the snow with an effortless grace that merely emphasized his own clumsiness.*

*Clumsy or not, he had to keep going. He had to get away. The flashlight sputtered and Danny knew the battery wouldn't last much longer. He had to find his way out of here before he was left in total darkness.*

*He dared to glance backwards towards the sound of the skier behind him, only to realize the sounds were now coming from the front. Or were they coming from the side? Was more than one thing out there, closing in on him from all sides?*

*Frozen in place, his eyes darted from left to right as he tried to decide the safest direction to move. The howl of a wolf made him jump and start moving again before he made a decision. The important thing was to keep going. Any direction would do. Danny yelled out as he stumbled over something in his path and fell on all fours into the snow.*

*He dropped the flashlight and watched it disappear into the snow. Danny reached forward with his hand to find out what had tripped him and froze as his fingers touched human flesh.*

*To his amazement, he no longer needed his flashlight. The moon had emerged full in the sky and cast a silver glow over the snow around him. And a glow over the arm his fingers touched.*

*Danny leaned back on his haunches and stifled a scream. In front of him lay a blond woman dressed in an emerald green Victorian gown. Her long blond hair had been piled on her head and now formed a golden halo around her face in the snow. Blood dripped from her neck and speckled the white landscape with spots of bright red. She looked so familiar....*

*Danny stood up and started to back away from the body. He needed to call this in to the station. He needed backup. He froze again as he heard the gliding sound return, closer now. And the moon had disappeared, plunging him back into darkness. Where was his flashlight? A beam of light to his left caught his eye.*

*"Are you looking for this?"*

*Aleksei held Danny's flashlight in his hand. The wind rippled through his blond hair as his dark blue eyes met Danny's gaze.*

*"You..." Danny took more steps backwards. "Stay away from me. Stay the hell away from me!"*

*He fell back into the snow and within seconds, Aleksei, towered over him.*

*"Stay away from you? Why didn't you stay away from me? You were never meant to find Maria..."*

*"Get back!"*

*Aleksei laughed and leaned closer to Danny. He smiled, revealing his fangs.*

*"What are you so afraid of, Detective?"*

*"Stay away!"*

Danny jumped and sat straight up in bed. His sheets were a knotted mess at his feet and his pillow lay crumpled in a ball on the floor. Sox sat at the foot of the bed and stared at him with cocked ears and a puzzled expression on his face

Danny gulped in air and looked around his Fairbanks bedroom, trying to convince himself that his surroundings were real. He wasn't in the Arctic and it wasn't winter. As if trying to help Danny get his bearings, Sox padded up to him and licked his face.

He reached out to pet the dog with a trembling hand.

"That's a good boy," he said. "You must be getting used to this by now."

## Polar Day

Danny continued to take deep breaths until his heart returned to a normal beat and his hands stopped shaking. The nightmares had been increasing steadily over the past few weeks, and last night's case had done nothing to keep them at bay.

Glancing over at his bedside table, Danny looked at his clock and was amazed to see it was only 11:00 a.m. He'd only been asleep for three hours. But that was three hours too many. If there was one thing Danny hated now, it was sleep.

He rolled out of bed and went straight to his kitchen to make a pot of coffee. As the coffee brewed and its scent filled the room, Danny headed for the bathroom and a scalding hot shower. It was time to go to work.

****

# Chapter 6

Danny strolled into the Fairbanks police department thirty minutes later with a thermos of coffee in one hand and a cold Pop-tart in the other. Bypassing his desk, he went straight to the department conference room, where he found Jack Meyer, Tessa and Anthony Rizzo already waiting for him.

"Morning, Danny," Tessa said.

His mouth full of blueberry Pop-tart, Danny nodded a greeting as he sat down at the table. He swallowed his breakfast, took a sip of coffee and immediately stood up again to cross the room and open a row of windows. To his dismay, the hot air outside did nothing to ease the stifling air in the room.

"Why don't you people in this state believe in central air?" he asked as he sat back down in his chair.

"You know how many days we normally need it?" Jack answered, wiping the sweat that had beaded on his brow. "Christ, half the time we don't even get above 70 degrees in the summer. Why the hell would we need central air conditioning?"

"We need it this summer," Danny said. "We could at least get a window unit."

"Fitzpatrick, can we talk about this poor bastard that burned to a crisp last night or do you have more to say about your own discomfort?" Jack asked.

Jack was a large man, with a booming voice to match his size. His face was perpetually red, or at least it seemed to be whenever he was around Danny. Danny was well aware that he irritated his boss to no end but he made no effort to change the situation.

He took another bite of Pop-tart and waved his hand in a dismissive gesture. "By all means, let's talk about the poor bastard. What do we know?"

Anthony Rizzo spoke up. "Not much, I'm afraid. We haven't been able to find any sign of an accelerant or a combustible substance on the remains or in the area."

"The flames were white when Tessa and I got to the body," Danny said. "That indicates the hottest temperature, right?"

"Sure does. You're talking over 2,000 degrees Fahrenheit right there." Rizzo paused. "So far we've done preliminary tests looking for liquids with low auto-ignition points, meaning they'll start on fire without any kind of accelerant. Keep in mind though, there's no auto-ignition point that's anywhere near as close to a normal air temperature even on a hot night like last night, but I don't know where else to start. I'll be honest, none of this makes a damn bit of sense."

"What did we get from the interviews?" Jack asked.

Danny answered first. "I talked to the two kids who were sneaking into the woods for a make-out session right before the fire started. They both said they saw a shadow in front of the runner before he grabbed his throat and appeared to be choking, but then the figure disappeared. I'd think they were just seeing things if I hadn't seen it too, like I told you last night."

"Yeah, I remember. But what the hell was it?"

"I don't know. A shadow, like the kids said. Honest to God, that's all I saw too. It looked like a figure in shadow. I thought it was a trick of the light because of the sun still being so high in the sky. Wouldn't thought a thing of it if what came next hadn't happened."

"Anybody else report seeing anything?"

"No," Tessa said.

"Nothing," Danny said. "The only thing of interest I got was the kids saying they heard chanting before the fire started."

"What was that about again?" Jack asked.

"The two teenagers who were closest to the fire when it started both told me they heard a man's voice chanting something. They felt like the voice was coming from right in front of the jogger but they couldn't see anyone."

"What was the man chanting?"

"They couldn't say. They said the chants were in a foreign language and they couldn't guess what it was. The kids said they know French and Spanish so it wasn't either one of those. The boy said the words sounded harsh."

"Well where in hell was the guy who was chanting?"

"They never saw anyone. I didn't see anyone either." Danny shrugged his shoulders. "It's another mystery. What about the surveillance cameras at the park? Or the cell phone videos? Anything useful there?"

Jack sighed. "We're pulling together the cell phone footage but so far all anyone recorded is the fire itself. That and selfies of themselves at the game before the fire started. But honestly there's not much. Only a few people recorded the fire. Almost everyone there was too stunned and horrified to remember to turn their damn cameras on and record that poor stiff burning to death. I've got guys going over the surveillance cameras now too but none were focused on that area of the track. I don't think we're going to get anything from them. And I went through the uniforms' reports from last night and they didn't get anything either. Not a damn thing that could point us to a lead. All we've got is some unseen person chanting and Fitzpatrick's shadow thing, which means we've got shit. No offense, Fitzpatrick."

"None taken. But don't forget the kids saw it too. It could mean something, if we can figure out who or what it was."

Jack turned back to Anthony Rizzo. "Have you heard anything on the identification of this guy? Do we know who he is? Or was?"

Rizzo shook his head. "No. Forensics was able to get partial prints and we're waiting for a match on those."

"They got fingerprints from that?" Danny asked. "How?"

"The victim was in what's called the fighter's stance – fingers clenched, arms up. It's what bodies do when they're burning. The balled up hands usually allow for fingerprints, at least partial ones."

"No one has called in to report a family member or friend going jogging last night and not coming home," Tessa said.

"It seemed like half the city was at that game last night," Danny said. "Everyone must have heard about this by now. Somebody must know the guy."

Jack sighed. "With luck we'll get a call on a missing person. Or a match on those prints." He rubbed his eyes with beefy fingers. "Christ what a mess."

"What could have started that fire?" Tessa asked Anthony.

"Honestly, I don't know. All I can figure is somebody tossed something combustible onto the trail and since everything is so dry because of this heat it caught fire. Maybe something as simple as a burning cigarette."

"You really think a cigarette could have started a fire that intense in such a short time? The way those flames engulfed that poor guy, it seemed like someone poured gasoline all over him and then tossed a match," Tessa said. "I've never seen a fire like that. I almost got burned myself just standing next to it."

"The guy was rolling in the grass to try to put the fire out while Tessa and I were running towards him," Danny said. "Didn't make a damn bit of difference. If anything, the flames just got worse."

"So much for stop, drop and roll," Jack said.

Anthony shook his head. "I know it doesn't add up," he said. "But I can't find any explanation that does."

"Let's go back to the interviews," Jack said. "Anybody acting strange when you talked to them? Maybe overly excited? We know arsonists love to hang around the scene of their handiwork."

"I didn't pick up on anything like that," Danny said. "Everyone I talked to just seemed to be in shock."

"Same here," Tessa said.

"I don't really know what we can do here," Jack said. "We don't even know if this is a homicide or some kind of freak accident."

"Or even a freak of nature," Anthony said.

Jack raised his eyebrows. "Meaning?"

Anthony shrugged his shoulders. "Spontaneous human combustion?"

"Is that real?" Tessa asked. "I know I've heard of it but I've always thought there must be some rational explanation for the fire that people just can't discover."

Danny stared at the table and remained silent. He didn't know anything about spontaneous human combustion, but he knew there were things that defied rational explanation. In the past, he would have scoffed at the idea of spontaneous human combustion and questioned its existence just like Tessa. But thanks to Aleksei Nechayev, there wasn't anything he scoffed at now.

"Christ Almighty," Jack said. "I don't even want to go there. Let's just wait for the report from the ME. I don't know what else we can do for now."

Danny and Tessa started to get up from the table when Jack stopped them.

"Fitzpatrick, I need to talk to you for a minute."

Danny sat back down in his chair.

"You two are free to go," Jack said, gesturing at Tessa and Anthony.

Danny watched his colleagues leave the room and turned back to his boss.

"Did I do something to piss you off again?" he asked.

"No, no," Jack said, shaking his head. "I wanted to let you know I got a report from the FBI team up in the Arctic."

A chill took over Danny's body in spite of the heat in the room.

"You know Fairbanks isn't the only part of the state under a heat wave," his boss continued. "It's warmer than usual up there too. The snow melt is helping them with their investigation."

"How so?" Danny asked, not really wanting to know the answer.

"They've turned up three more bodies. All young women. The cold and the ice left them remarkably preserved."

Danny nodded. "Have they ID'd them?"

"One of them. They found your old case. Anna Alexander."

Danny's throat closed up. Anna was the reason he had stumbled upon Aleksei Nechayev. Her resemblance to another missing woman, Maria Treibel, had sent Danny sniffing in Aleksei's direction. He'd followed his gut instinct that the two women were connected, never imagining where that instinct would ultimately lead him.

"I hope that will give her parents some peace," he said, a catch in his voice.

"Here's the crazy thing," Jack said. "They said one of these bodies had been up there for at three or four decades. Obviously not one of Nechayev's victims. But I wonder if he was copying some other piece of shit when he started all this."

No, Danny thought. Whoever she was, she was one of Aleksei's victims too. But there was no way Danny could explain Aleksei's real age and decades of crime to his boss.

"I guess we'll never know, sir," he said.

"Of course, they haven't found Nechayev himself. Or the dead girl from Seattle. No sign of Katie."

Danny tried his best not to grimace as he recalled that dead girl flashing her fangs at him while she prepared to leave Alaska with Aleksei. She was Katya now. While Katie was most definitely dead, Katya was not. She was a monster, just like her creator Aleksei.

"I doubt we'll ever find Nechayev," Danny said.

"So you've said. But I think that's just the trauma talking, Fitzpatrick. There's no way in hell he could have gotten out of the Arctic alive. We'll find his body eventually."

Danny flashed back to the postcard he had received from the vampire a few months earlier. At that time, he and Katya had been in Aleksei's hometown of St. Petersburg in Russia. Danny had no doubt they were long gone from there by now. He wondered how many residents of St. Petersburg had fallen victim to them before they'd left.

"Are you alright?" Jack asked.

Danny forced a smile onto his pale face. "Fine, sir. All of this just brings back bad memories."

"Of course it does. But I thought you'd want to know."

"I do. And I appreciate the update." Danny got up from his chair and lifted his coffee cup from the table. "Do you need me for anything else?"

Jack shook his head. "No."

Danny nodded and left the room.

Jack watched him leave and wondered, not for the first time, if he had made a mistake promoting Danny to homicide. He didn't doubt his excellent detective skills; Fitzpatrick had proven those and then some when he'd solved the Nechayev case, but Jack knew the man had been emotionally fragile even before he'd nearly been killed in Nechayev's Arctic home. By all accounts, Danny was managing well now and had even sobered up, something Jack would never have believed possible just a few months before. But he knew the stress of homicide could sometimes unhinge even the most stable detective.

Jack had seen the shadow cross over Danny's face as soon as he had mentioned the Arctic. It was obvious the man wasn't over what had happened to him. Jack doubted he ever would be.

****

# Chapter 7

Jamie Dzubenko sat at his lab table and tried to focus on the slide under the microscope in front of him. In spite of the fact that he'd had three cups of coffee in the last hour, he was having trouble keeping his eyes open. Last night had been exhilarating beyond his wildest dreams, but it had also been more exhausting than he ever could have imagined.

It continued to surprise him that the invisible spell took nearly as much energy as the fire spell. He had assumed nothing would require as much focus and concentration as creating fire out of thin air, but he'd been wrong. It turned out most of his spells required the same amount of stamina. In short, they were all exhausting on their own and nearly crippling when performed together.

But oh my, were they ever worth it. Jamie's plans for the Midnight Sun baseball game had gone off without a hitch, and he was still walking on air as he remembered the chaos and destruction he'd unleashed. The burning man had been even more spectacular than his first victim and seeing the revelry of the idiots at the game turn to terror had been one of the biggest thrills of Jamie's life.

"Dzubenko?"

The sound of his boss calling his name snapped Jamie out of his own revelry.

"Over here," he answered, quickly pretending to be concentrating while staring through his microscope.

Stephen Ramey, his supervisor in the Fairbanks hospital medical technology lab, came to his side.

"Do you have the results for patient Tu643?" Ramey asked, checking the number with the paper on his clipboard.

Jamie turned to his computer and quickly typed in his password to bring up his log. "Sure," he said, scanning the screen in front of him. "Positive, I'm afraid. Let me print this out for you."

Polar Day

He printed out the results and handed them to his boss. "Anything else?"

Ramey shook his head. "No, not now." He held up the paper before walking away. "Thanks for getting this so quickly."

"Not a problem."

As always, Jamie was relieved to be left alone. While he had no interest in the patients whose lab work he routinely performed, he loved his job. For as long as he could remember, he'd loved science. Even during the darkest and most mundane days of his childhood, he'd loved chemistry and biology. Test tubes and specimens were infinitely more interesting to him than people had ever been. Once he'd aged out of foster care and needed a way to take care of himself he'd stumbled upon medical technology and knew he'd found the perfect field. Now, Jamie spent his days alone in his lab with his science and his nights alone with his plans.

When Jamie had stumbled upon the secret his family had kept hidden for decades he was sure it was too good to be true. It seemed impossible that he possessed the ability to take his beloved science to a whole new and surreal level. His parents had tried to hide the magic that was rightfully his from him, but Jamie had not put up with that for long. He'd never allowed his parents or his siblings to stand in his way. He had made sure of that.

The power had been exhilarating since the very first time he had tried it out as a child, even when he had no idea what he was saying while chanting the spells. As he'd grown older and learned to read the Ukrainian texts his great-grandfather had brought with him from his homeland, the power became intoxicating. Jamie knew he was someone special.

But he was edgy now in addition to being exhausted. After being interviewed by one of the stunned Fairbanks detectives at the ball field and dutifully expressing his own shock and terror, Jamie had left Growden Park to return to the scene of his first triumph in Griffin Park the previous month. As he'd suspected, the park was empty, as anyone in Fairbanks who hadn't already been at the baseball game had run to witness the chaos for themselves upon hearing the news of the fire. Jamie had Griffin Park to himself.

The sun had finally set by the time he arrived and he tried in vain to suppress his glee as he made use of the few hours of twilight before the sun made its return. This was as dark as it got in Fairbanks during the summer. Jamie knew exactly where he had hidden his first victim last month and he was thrilled to see that Max Fugate's remains had not yet been found. He assumed they hadn't since he hadn't heard anything on the news about such a gruesome discovery, but it was still a relief to know for sure that his plan was going to play out exactly as he wanted it to. It took only minutes to brush away the leaves and sticks that hid the charred corpse from passers-by. Jamie only wished he could be on the scene to see the terror on some unsuspecting jogger's face when they came upon such a macabre and horrifying sight as they trotted along the trail.

Now, Jamie repeatedly refreshed the Fairbanks news websites looking for word of the discovery. Surely someone would find the remains today. The timing had to be perfect.

Jamie's lips curled into a smile as he refreshed a page yet again and saw a breaking news bulletin flash at the top. Now that he finally had what he was waiting for, his exhaustion was quickly forgotten.

He had been preparing for years for this, and it was starting now. This summer, Fairbanks was going to see his masterpiece.

****

# Chapter 8

"Oh my Lord," Tessa said, echoing the thoughts of all who stood around the blackened human remains that had been discovered an hour earlier by a jogger in Griffin Park.

Danny remained silent, unable to form any words that would do justice to the fear that was threatening to overtake him. With the previous night's horror so fresh in his mind that he could still smell the burning flesh, the body in front of them now was too much to process. He stared at the carnage at his feet and heard the voice and the laughter of Aleksei Nechayev in his mind.

"What kind of monster are you dealing with now, Detective? I was never the only one, you knew that, right?"

"Danny, are you okay?"

Danny heard Tessa's voice and wondered why she sounded so far away when the last he'd noticed she'd been standing right next to him.

"Danny? What's wrong?"

He felt Tessa's hand on his arm and looked down at her as the sound of Nechayev's laughter disappeared.

"Nothing," he said. "I'm fine. Just spaced out for a minute I guess."

Danny could feel Jack Meyer's eyes on him. The captain had been pressuring him to take advantage of the department's counseling services ever since the Nechayev case. Danny had consistently refused. Not wanting to give his boss any reason to push the counseling again, Danny forcefully banished all thoughts of the vampire from his mind and put on his game face.

"Where's the woman who found the body?" he asked.

Tessa pointed in the direction of a young woman who was doubled over against a nearby tree. She had clearly vomited several times and now clutched her stomach.

"I'm gonna go talk to her," Danny said, anxious to be away from the corpse.

"Ma'am," he said as he walked up beside the woman. "Are you okay? Do you need me to get the paramedics over here?"

The woman stood up and ran her fingers through her short, spiky blond hair, causing it to stick out in all directions. Her face was so pale it was nearly translucent and her thin lips trembled as she stared at Danny with puffy and tear-filled eyes.

"I'm okay," she said.

Danny held out his hand. "I'm Detective Danny Fitzpatrick, Fairbanks PD. If you're up to it, I'd like to talk with you about what happened here."

The woman nodded and returned Danny's handshake with a clammy and trembling hand. "That's fine."

"What's your name?"

"Emily Schumacher."

"Do you jog here often, Ms. Schumacher?"

"Almost every morning. This is my favorite park."

"I like it too," Danny said. "I bring my dog here a lot. Were you here yesterday? On this same trail?"

"Yes. I've been here every day this week. I come here to run before I go in to work. I'm a nurse and work second shift at Fairbanks General."

"Did you see anyone else jogging or walking here this morning?"

Emily shook her head. "No. I had the park to myself."

Danny kept quiet, watching Emily stare at the corpse and the medical examiners who had now shown up to do their work.

"I was jogging and noticed piles of branches and leaves off to the side of the trail. I glanced over and saw that," she said, pointing at the corpse with a shaking hand.

"But you didn't see anyone else around? Maybe ahead of you on the trail?"

"No."

"How long had you been jogging?"

"About 15 minutes I guess." She gestured around her. "This is the halfway point of the trail."

Danny was aware of that. It was also the point farthest from the entrance to the park and the passing street.

"What about any weird noises? Did you hear anything strange while you were jogging?"

"Nothing. I'm sorry, I just..." Emily shook her head again. "There was nothing."

"You don't have anything to be sorry for."

Emily slid down the trunk of the tree and sat on the grass.

"Do you think this is connected to that jogger who died at the game last night?"

"I couldn't say."

A uniformed officer Danny recognized as a young rookie named Randy approached with a plastic cup of water in his hand.

"Detective?" he asked. "Can I take the witness's statement?"

"Of course," Danny said. "And I think she could use that water too, good idea." He nodded towards Emily, who remained on the grass. "Thanks for answering my questions."

Danny walked back over to Tessa and Jack, who were now conferring with Joanna Mickens, the chief medical examiner. He nodded a greeting to Mickens.

"Joanna," he said.

"Hello, Danny. I was just telling your colleagues here that my preliminary estimate is that this body's been here for at least two weeks, probably more like a month."

Danny glanced at the pile of branches Emily Schumacher had initially noticed. "So someone covered this body up with all that crap so it would be hidden from anyone coming by on the trail. And then that same someone dug the body up last night or this morning so someone using the trail would find it."

"That's a safe bet," Jack said.

"Did he burn to death?" Danny asked. "Or is it a she? Do you know?"

"It's a male. But as for the cause of death, I can't say for sure," Joanna said. "We'll need to examine the remains to determine whether he was still alive when he burned. It's possible he was killed another way and then the body was burned."

"But not all that likely considering what happened last night," Tessa said. "We all know this isn't a coincidence."

"Christ let's not jump ahead of ourselves," Jack said. "I may agree with you that this timing would be one hell of a coincidence but let's take it slowly. We all need to get a grip."

Anthony Rizzo walked up to the group, looking even more exhausted and disheartened than he had that morning in the conference room. Danny had no doubt that Rizzo hated life right now and wished he'd been able to retire six months earlier.

"There are signs of a relatively recent grass fire not far from the grave," he said, pointing towards a few weeds and ferns sticking out of a patch of dirt along the jogging trail. "The weeds are starting to come back but the ground is charred. I can't find any traces of an accelerant or combustible material on it though. It was contained to that small circle."

"Why wouldn't it have spread?" Danny asked. "We haven't had any rain in months, have we? This grass all looks really dry."

"Someone must have put it out before it spread."

"It's strange that it's such a small area," Tessa said.

Anthony's expression showed his agreement. "It is," he said.

"As strange as last night's situation," Danny said.

"Goddammit, Fitzpatrick. I just said we don't need to get ahead of ourselves," Jack said, glancing over at approaching reporters. "You want the media to get a hold of this and turn it into a fiasco?"

"I'd say it's already a fiasco, sir," Danny said. "You know it too."

Jack glared at Danny but the ringing of his phone stopped him from responding. He grabbed the phone from his pocket and turned his back on Danny.

"Meyer," he said. "Yeah? What's the name? Okay, we'll get on it."

Jack turned back to the group. "That was the station. A man named Andrew Cushings called from Anchorage and said his partner Nick Torrance is here in Fairbanks for an IT conference. Last he talked to him Torrance said he was going jogging in Growden Park. I probably don't have to tell you this was last night. Cushings hasn't heard from him since and he's not answering his phone or the phone in his hotel room."

"What's his partner look like?" Danny asked.

"Tall, fit, gray hair…"

"That matches the jogger I saw before he started to burn."

Polar Day

Tessa frowned. "Where was he staying?"

"The Marriott on Bentley. He told his partner he wanted to check out the baseball game while he was jogging."

"You want us to head over there?"

"Yeah. I'll handle this here and we'll meet back up at the office. And let's start looking through last month's missing person reports. With luck maybe we can figure out who this poor bastard is too."

\*\*\*\*

# Chapter 9

While Tessa drove, Danny took out his iPad and logged into the police department files. He quickly brought up the missing persons reports made during the previous month.

"So all we know is we're looking for a male, right?" he said.

"Well, we can guess he was probably jogging since he was so close to the trail."

"What the hell does this lunatic have against joggers?"

"It's weird, isn't it? Although we don't know for sure that these cases are connected."

"Oh, come on, Tessa."

"You know I think they are too. I'm just saying it could still be a coincidence."

"Right. And Nick Torrance could still be alive and simply hiding from his partner."

"He could be," Tessa said.

Danny rolled his eyes. They had found nothing of interest in the hotel room of Nick Torrance, but the fact that his cell phone and wallet were gone, his work clothes and laptop remained in the hotel room, he hadn't shown up for his scheduled conference that morning, and no one in the hotel had seen him since he left to go jogging the previous evening told a fairly clear story. As did the missing persons reports.

While the number of people who went missing in Alaska could be high due to the vastness and remoteness of the state, the number of people reported missing in Fairbanks was usually minuscule. The majority of cases were closed within a few days of being opened because the missing person turned up safe and sound, unaware that he or she had even been considered missing.

Danny skimmed through reports made in the month of May and landed on one that was still open.

"Max Fugate," he said.

"What?"

"A guy named Max Fugate was reported missing on May 24 after he didn't show up for work at the Fairbanks hospital. He was a doctor so a lot of people noticed when he didn't show. His sister went to his home and all of his belongings were there but he wasn't. No one could get in touch with him on his cell. The last known contact with him was with his neighbor who said he told her on the night of the 23rd that he was going jogging in Griffin Park."

"Oh my," Tessa said. "Sounds like our guy, doesn't it?"

"Sure does. Poor guy."

"Well if he was a doctor he'll have fingerprints on file at the hospital. Maybe they'll be able to get prints from the body and identify him that way."

"Maybe. I wonder if his hands were balled up the way Anthony mentioned this morning."

"Yeah, what did he call that, the fighter's stance? Never heard of that before."

"I hadn't either. Wish I still hadn't heard of it."

"Agree with you there," Tessa said.

She pulled into the police station lot and found a spot near the front entrance. The two detectives squinted in the blazing sun as they got out of the car.

"Jesus I wish we could stay in the car in the air conditioning," Danny said.

Tessa wiped beads of sweat from her forehead. "Agree with you again. This heat has to let up soon."

"I feel like we've been saying that for weeks."

"In all these years I've never felt heat like this in Alaska before. Never anything close."

Danny walked to the door and held it open for his partner to walk inside.

"You're such a gentleman, Danny," Tessa said, smiling in spite of the uncomfortable heat.

"My mother taught me well."

Tessa laughed. "Something tells me your mother would shudder to see most of what you get yourself up to."

"Something tells me you're right. Now let's head into our furnace of an office and see if we can match Mr. Fugate with that corpse in the park."

****

# Chapter 10

"I read about the fire up there at the baseball game," Amanda said. "Is that your case?"

"Yes it is," Danny said. "Tessa and I were both there and saw the whole thing."

"Oh my God. I can't imagine it."

"No, I doubt you can. Consider yourself fortunate."

Danny plopped onto his couch and opened a beer as he cradled his phone between his shoulder and his ear. Sox jumped up next to him and turned in a circle three times before settling down with his head in Danny's lap. Danny set his beer on the end table next to him and scratched the dog's ears.

"So how's your mom?" he asked.

Amanda had been in her hometown of Sitka for the past few weeks helping to care for her mother, who had suffered a devastating heart attack. Danny had alternated between missing her company and feeling relief that he was on his own. He cared for Amanda, but didn't see the relationship progressing to anything beyond friendship. While they'd never discussed it, he was fairly certain that Amanda felt the same way.

Still, the two shared a bond that would never go away, as Amanda was the only person besides Danny who knew the truth about Aleksei Nechayev. As the only known person to survive an attack by Aleksei prior to Maria Treibel, Amanda had been the one to convince Danny of Aleksei's true nature early on in the Nechayev case. She had also saved his life by convincing his colleagues of the need to rescue him from Aleksei's clutches following his decision to venture into the Arctic and confront Nechayev on his own.

"She's getting a little better," Amanda said. "Still a long way to go though. I can't believe how weak and frail she is."

"I'm sure she and your dad are both glad you're there with them."

"Yeah, I think so. Maybe this is a chance for us to be close again."

Amanda's relationship with her family had become strained following Aleksei's attack and her insistence that he was not human.

Her parents didn't believe her, a fact that had caused Amanda to leave Sitka for Fairbanks. She had never forgiven her parents for their doubts about her sanity, in spite of the fact that she understood how crazy her vampire assertions had seemed.

"I hope so," Danny said.

"I'm considering staying here through the summer. Between my vacation time and the family medical leave I can swing it at work. My boss doesn't have a problem with it."

"I think that's a good idea. Your mom's what's important right now."

Danny took a swig of beer and switched to scratching Sox's chin instead of his ears. The dog protested and burrowed his head into Danny's leg in an effort to force him to leave his chin alone and return to his ears. The dog quickly won and Danny relented.

"How are you doing, Danny? Still having the dreams?"

"Sometimes. I had one the other night. It was the same thing – the woman in the snow, Aleksei standing over me with his fangs out..."

"Have you had any more contact from him?"

"No, thankfully."

Danny had confided in Amanda about the postcard he had received from Nechayev back in March. At that time, the vampire and his companion Katerina were in St. Petersburg, Russia. Danny had alerted the St. Petersburg police about the possibility of a dangerous fugitive in their city and immediately felt guilty about doing so. Sending them into Nechayev's clutches surely endangered their own lives, and there was little hope that they could end Nechayev's. Danny could hardly convince the police that they needed wooden stakes instead of guns to apprehend Aleksei.

While he knew it was cowardly, Danny had purposefully avoided any news of St. Petersburg following his call to their police. If there had been a bloody massacre of police officers in the time following his call he didn't want to know about it. And he had kept silent about the postcard except with Amanda. His guilt increased as the FBI continued their search for Nechayev in the Alaskan Arctic, but Danny didn't dare tell anyone the reason he knew their efforts were in vain. He knew no one would believe him and he couldn't afford to lose his job over what would surely be considered mental illness if he pressed the issue.

"This new case has me on edge though," he continued. "I can't help thinking if it's something else that isn't quite of this world."

"You mean the fire?"

"Yeah. I saw something right before the guy started burning. It was like a shadow in front of him. Some nearby kids saw it too. And they heard chanting but couldn't see anyone around who could be doing it."

"Chanting? So you think there might be some kind of magic involved?"

Danny downed his beer and stood up to walk to his kitchen for another bottle. Sox grumbled his disapproval but remained on the couch, ready for his scratching to resume as soon as Danny returned.

"Christ I don't know. I hate even thinking it. But Rizzo, the arson investigator, said he couldn't find a damn thing on the remains or at the scene that could have started the fire in the usual ways. No accelerant, nothing combustible..."

He returned to the couch and drank nearly half the bottle before sitting back down. He had brought a third one that he set on the table. A case like this made him forget his vow to cut back on his drinking.

"Then today we found another burned body," he said. "You probably haven't seen anything about that yet. They're trying to keep it away from the media."

"No, I hadn't."

"Well you will soon enough. According to the M.E. the guy was probably killed about a month ago and covered up with sticks and branches so he wouldn't be found. Whoever's responsible for this dug him up so we'd find him now after the baseball game fire."

"Oh my goodness."

Danny let out a bitter laugh. "Yeah. It's a real mess." He took another swallow of beer. "So since you're the monster expert..."

"I'm not an expert. Just because I knew what Aleksei was..."

"You're the closest thing I know to an expert, okay? Do you think there are fire monsters of some kind? Demonic creatures that go around setting people on fire like Aleksei and his kind drain them of their blood?"

"I've never heard of anything like that. But..." Amanda paused.

"But what?"

"But like I asked before when you mentioned the chanting the kids heard at the game. Could it be some kind of magic?"

"What, like spells? Witchcraft?"

"Maybe."

"Oh my God."

"I don't know. I don't know anything about magic. It just came to my mind when you said those kids heard chanting."

Danny could picture Amanda as she talked, her fingers nervously clutching the silver crucifix she always wore around her neck.

"Well you were right last time about the vampire so I wouldn't be surprised if you're right now, too," he said. "But I really hope you're not. God almighty. How the hell am I supposed to work this?"

"I'm sure I'm wrong. The arson guy will find a rational explanation for what's happened. Just give it some time."

"Yeah, well, Rizzo doesn't exactly inspire confidence, believe me. He's retiring in a few months and I can tell this whole situation is killing him. He can't believe he's stuck with it when he thought he'd spend the summer counting the days until he walked out of the station for the last time. Not that I blame him. I'd feel the same way in his shoes."

Danny heard a man's voice on the other side of the line.

"Is that your dad?" he asked.

"Yeah. He needs some help getting Mom up."

"You go ahead then. I'll talk to you soon."

"You take care of yourself. Don't let this case get to you."

"Easier said than done."

"I know but please try. And say hi to Sox for me, okay?"

"That part is easy. You take care of yourself too."

Danny set his phone down on the table and lifted Sox's snout to his face.

"Amanda says hello."

The dog's ears perked up at Amanda's name and he checked around the room to make sure he had not missed her entrance.

"No, she's not here. She said hello over the phone."

No longer recognizing the words, Sox plopped his face back down on Danny's legs.

Danny chuckled and pushed the dog aside so he could get up from the couch. He walked to the kitchen and returned with two more bottles of beer. He grabbed the television remote before sitting back down on the couch.

"What do you want to watch, Sox?"

The dog thumped his tail against the couch cushion in response.

Danny flipped through the channels, stopping when he came to a Seattle Mariners game that had gone in to extra innings. They were playing the White Sox in Chicago and Danny felt a slight tug at his heartstrings as the familiar sight of Cellular Field filled the flat screen television. The time difference made it difficult for him to catch Sox games live. It was a welcome surprise to find one that was lasting so long into the Chicago night that he could watch it live as it happened.

It was dark in Chicago, but of course the sun was still high in the sky here in this strange frontier he had chosen as his new home. He squinted from the sun beaming through the window and cursed himself for not shutting the blinds before he sat back down. Next time he got up for a beer he would need to do that.

Danny rested his hand on his dog's head as he finished one beer and started another, the bottles now lining up on the end table beside him. His eyes grew bleary as Sox's gentle snoring mingled with the sounds of the faraway baseball game. When yet another inning ended and the game went to a commercial, Danny closed his eyes and rested his head on the back of the couch.

The noise of the television grew fainter as he slipped into sleep and his mind flashed images of fangs and bloodless bodies in an endless landscape of snow. As Danny drifted farther into unconsciousness, the snow was overtaken by fire.

****

# Chapter 11

"You look like hell."

"Thank you, Tessa," Danny said as he set his thermos of coffee on his desk. "I can always count on you to brighten my morning."

"Were you up drinking?"

"No," Danny lied. "I was watching a baseball game and fell asleep on the couch. If I look like hell it's likely because I've got a crick in my neck from sleeping upright all night." He grabbed a tissue from Tessa's desk and wiped the sweat from his forehead. "And because it's hotter than hell in here."

Tessa sipped from a cup of ice water on her desk. "It is, can't argue with you there."

"Anything new on our guys?"

"The body found yesterday was Max Fugate. They were able to get fingerprints that matched his file at the hospital. Nick Torrance was arrested on a DUI charge years ago in Anchorage, so his prints are on file too if they can get them from what remains of his hands. Apparently they're still working on that."

"What about the autopsy report? Was Fugate burned alive too?"

"Yeah."

"Jesus Christ. Anything else was too much to hope for, wasn't it?"

"I think so."

Danny sat down at his desk. "What else do we know about him?"

"He's a Fairbanks native and his parents and sister also live here. He wasn't married and had no children."

"So I guess we start with the parents and the sister. Have they been notified?"

Tessa shook her head. "No, the ID just came in. You and I are the lucky ones who get to do that."

"Goddammit." Danny let out a breath. "I hate this shit."

"Who doesn't?"

Tessa got up from her chair. "You driving or am I?"

"I'll drive."

"Excuse me, officers?"

Danny and Tessa turned to see Mark Chambers, the desk sergeant, holding an envelope out to them.

"Yeah?" Danny asked.

"This just came in the mail. I'm not sure if I should give it to you or to Captain Meyer. It's addressed to homicide detectives."

Tessa took the envelope. "We've got it. Thanks, Mark."

She laid the envelope on her desk. There was no return address and the address of the police station was printed in pencil with a neat and precise penmanship. The postmark said Fairbanks and showed the letter had been mailed the day before.

"I don't like this," Tessa said.

"I don't either."

Danny pulled some gloves from the drawer of his desk and picked up the envelope.

"Let's bring it to the boss."

The two walked to Jack Meyer's office and knocked. The captain was talking on the phone but motioned for them to enter.

Jack quickly hung up the phone and glanced up at the detectives. "What's up?"

Danny held out the envelope and placed it on Meyer's desk. "We just received a strange envelope."

The captain looked at the letter and reached into his own desk drawer for gloves. He picked the envelope up and gingerly opened it with a letter opener. He turned the envelope upside down and let one sheet of paper fall onto the desk.

The paper was plain white and the words "Who do you think is next?" were written at the top of the page in the same penmanship found on the envelope. An old image of the advertising mascot Smoky Bear standing in front of a raging fire was printed underneath the words.

"Oh my God," Tessa said.

"It looks like someone wants to have some fun with us," Danny said.

The three stared at the paper in front of them, all momentarily speechless.

"We need to get forensics on this," Jack finally said. He picked up the phone and barked out some orders before slamming the receiver back down. "Were you two heading out to notify Fugate's next of kin?"

"Yes," Tessa said.

"We'll get some uniforms to do it. We need all of us on this now." He rubbed his eyes and fell back into his chair, his eyes never leaving the paper on his desk. "Jesus fucking Christ."

"I'd say that about covers it," Danny said.

\*\*\*\*

# Chapter 12

Jennifer Higgins sat at her desk at Fairbanks Channel 10 news and scrolled through the police alerts on her desktop looking for something interesting to cover for her Emmy award winning "Crime Stoppers" feature. Of course, the fire at the Midnight Sun baseball game was still foremost in everyone's mind, but Jennifer was trying to find something everyone else wasn't already covering. Or an angle on the fire that fit the same criteria.

Like most of the city, she had been at the game and seen the horrifying spectacle with her own eyes. Despite years as a reporter and experience covering heinous crimes both here in Fairbanks and in her home town of Juneau, Jennifer had never seen anything as terrifying as the fire that had consumed the jogger at the baseball game. She hadn't been able to rein in her shock and regain her composure enough to view the scene as a reporter instead of as a bystander, something she was still angry at herself about. She might have been able to reel in another Emmy for her on the scene coverage if she had only acted like a professional instead of a shocked and frightened baseball fan.

She couldn't change that though and there was no point in dwelling on it. And no one even knew if the fire had been the result of a crime or simply a freak accident, so it was possible it didn't even fit her crime beat anyway.

Jennifer knew the police had been called to Griffin Park earlier in the day due to the discovery of a body there, but when she'd tried to go to the scene they'd had access completely blocked and neither she nor any of the rest of the media had been able to get anywhere near the area in question. Still, she'd figure out what happened soon enough. They couldn't block her access to the coroner's office or to the uniformed cops who were always willing to spill a few secrets about the ongoing cases of their superiors while they were hanging around one of the local

Julie Flanders

bars after work. Jennifer was an old hand at cajoling secrets out of men who had enough alcohol in them to loosen their tongues.

For now though she had nothing and worse yet could find nothing of interest to follow up on and cover. She supposed she would have no choice but to fall back on ongoing coverage of the baseball game fire for her segment that evening. It may be for the best as no one in town was talking about anything else anyway.

"This came for you, Jennifer."

Jennifer turned to see Peter Johnson, the man who had been delivering the station's mail since before she was born, standing next to her desk. He handed her an envelope.

"Thanks, Peter," she said. "How are you doing today?"

"Not bad. Except for this damn heat."

"It's miserable isn't it?"

"Sure is. If I wanted this kind of weather I would have moved to Florida a long time ago."

Jennifer laughed. "I hear ya. Try to keep cool."

"You too."

Jennifer smiled at Peter as he shuffled away from her desk. Like every place else, the station received less snail mail all the time. She hoped Peter would want to retire before the station decided to eliminate his position. She knew he was old enough to retire and had been for years, but he didn't seem to have much in his life besides his job. She hated to think of him being forced out.

She glanced at the white envelope he had given her and felt a twinge of alarm. Her name and the address of the station were hand-written in pencil and the envelope bore no return address. While it was probably nothing more than fan mail, which she and the rest of the anchors still received through the regular mail on occasion, something about the envelope made her uncomfortable.

When she opened it and took out the enclosed letter, she knew her instincts had been correct. "Who do you think is next?" was printed in large letters at the top of the page and underneath the question was a picture of Smokey the Bear at the scene of a fire. The image looked like one of the ads about preventing forest fires that she remembered so well from her childhood in the 1980s. She turned the paper over and found it blank.

## Polar Day

Jennifer set the letter on the desk in front of her and stared at the precisely written question. She could hear her heart pounding in her chest.

"Oh my," she said.

****

# Chapter 13

Jamie sat on the floor of his apartment wearing only his boxer shorts. He was thrilled to be working the night shift tonight so he could work on his rituals today. He needed the rejuvenation.

Keeping with the ancient customs of the Roman worshippers of Vulcan, he had hung all of his clothes outside on his patio to allow them to soak up the sun. He kept all the lights off in his apartment, which wasn't a hardship with the sun blazing through his windows, and surrounded himself with candles.

Sitting in a traditional yoga pose, Jamie placed his hands palms up on his knees. He closed his eyes and focused on regaining the peace and strength that the previous spells had taken out of him. It was difficult to focus, as he was so eager to know if the police detectives and the reporter had received his letters yet. Chances were good but he couldn't be sure. What he wouldn't give to be a fly on the walls of their offices.

But of course a mere fly was far beneath anything he already was and aspired to be.

Jamie had always found it revolting that his family had wasted the magic that had been their birthright. When he'd learned about the powers he had inherited from his great-grandfather, he couldn't believe neither his father nor his grandfather had ever made use of them. From what he could ascertain of his family history, his great-grandmother was the only member of his family who had respected the powers after her husband had been killed. She had been terrified of his book but had kept it in honor of the man who had last used the Dzubenko family magic. She had also tried to convince her son about the presence of the supernatural in the world, but he had dismissed her beliefs as nothing more than the ravings of a grief-stricken woman who had never recovered from the murder of her husband.

As a result, Jamie had nothing but contempt for his grandfather and his father for that matter. They had both turned their noses up at the idea of magic and the supernatural. He never would have learned about his gifts if he hadn't stumbled upon his great-grandfather's book in the attic of his childhood home. His parents had tried to dismiss his questions about the book but he'd been undeterred. He knew from the moment he'd opened the book that he was meant to have it. He knew that it was special. And he knew that he was too.

On the surface, Jamie didn't seem like anyone who would be called special. He was a small man with mousy brown hair, a sharp nose and beady eyes. It was a combination that gave him the look of a rodent. When he was younger he'd been teased and called more rat nicknames than he could remember. But none of that bothered him once he'd found the book. The book that showed him who, and what, he really was.

It had been a challenge to learn the Ukrainian language needed to understand the text, but he'd finally worked it out. As time went on, the magic somehow took over and he had become a master of the language despite never having any formal training. He'd fallen in love with the ancient words and phrases he could use to make magic. Above all, he'd fallen in love with the words he could use to make fire. It was through fire that Jamie had learned what he was meant to be.

After ridding himself of his family and childhood home, Jamie had immersed himself into the study of his ancestor's magic. He'd learned of the Ukrainian's ability to fight vampires and other creatures of the night through fire and other spells of black magic.

He'd also read the prophecies of Nostradamus and came across a prediction of a city gone bad that would need to be destroyed by Vulcan, the Roman god of fire. As Jamie had aged, his revulsion for the city of his birth had grown steadily. He believed it needed to be destroyed and that he was the man to do it. Through his magic, he could become a god and the modern day incarnation of Vulcan.

The power was intoxicating and Jamie felt more god-like with each spell he brought to fruition. He could feel the ancient power of Vulcan working through him and he almost pitied the cops who would task themselves with trying to stop him. Almost.

Mostly he felt contempt for them just as he felt contempt for the rest of the mindless robots wandering through this barren city. The cops would never be able to stop him and before the summer had ended the entire town of Fairbanks would be laid to waste. Jamie would be the only one left standing.

His plan had started better than he could ever have dreamed; convincing him even more that he was on the right path. Now his dream was becoming reality. And the fun was only just beginning.

\*\*\*\*

# Chapter 14

Danny and Tessa walked into the police conference room and sat down across from a frustrated Jack Meyer and an increasingly bedraggled Anthony Rizzo.

"What do we have?" Danny asked.

"We've got a shit storm is what we have," Jack said. "As you can expect, forensics couldn't find a single print on the letter. The words were written with a standard number two pencil that you can buy at any Walmart in the freaking world. The paper was the equally standard eight and a half by 11-inch 20-pound office paper. If you do a google search for Smokey the goddamn Bear you'll find the image our guy sent on more pages than I can count. We've got guys searching the IP addresses of visitors to the sites looking for a local connection, but right now it's a needle in a haystack."

"What about the postmark?" Tessa asked.

"It's the main Fairbanks branch downtown here. The letter was mailed yesterday. We're going over footage from the cameras inside the post office but unfortunately there aren't any cameras on the street outside where the mailboxes are. I don't think the cameras are going to give us shit anyway because this jackass could have used any number of mailboxes all over the city. They all go to the downtown branch." Jack paused and let out a breath. "Now tell me, do you two have anything? For once, please say yes."

"The prints on the baseball game victim matched Nick Torrance's old police record. He's our victim," Danny said.

"Alright so we've got Nick Torrance and Max Fugate. What do these two have in common?"

"So far, nothing," Tessa said. "Nick worked in IT and Max was a doctor. Max was a life-long Fairbanks resident and this convention was Nick's first visit here. They were obviously both joggers and both men, but other than that we haven't found anything."

"Torrance was gay, right?" Jack asked. "What about Fugate?"

"We don't know. We're getting ready to head out and talk to his family and colleagues," Danny said. "See what we can learn about him."

"Good," Jack said. "I need to set up a press conference too. We can't keep the media out of this much longer." He shook his head. "I just hate to start a panic. People are freaked out enough by the baseball game. Now when they hear about Fugate…"

"Honestly, sir, they're right to be afraid," Danny said. "People are being burned alive. Aren't we all freaked out?"

Jack scowled. "Of course we are, Fitzpatrick. But the police of all people don't need to start a panic, do they?"

A knock on the conference room door interrupted the meeting.

"Excuse me, Captain Meyer?"

Mark Chambers, the desk sergeant who had handed Tessa and Danny the envelope earlier was now at the door.

"Yes, what is it? We're in a meeting here."

"Sorry, sir, but Jennifer Higgins from Channel 10 is on the phone and says it's urgent she speak with a detective. She said it's about the baseball game fire."

Jack's scowl deepened. "Oh Christ here we go. God damn the media."

Danny stood up from his chair. "I'll talk with her. Jennifer and I go way back."

"You've only lived in Alaska for what, a goddamn year? How far back can you go?" Jack asked, his face reddening with each word.

"As long as I've been here," Danny said.

He left the room and headed for the main desk of the station. He liked Jennifer Higgins in spite of the fact that cops and reporters typically weren't pals. He had made a fool of himself while in a drunken stupor and hit on her at a local bar not long after he'd moved to Fairbanks. She hadn't been interested in his drunken advances and had actually tried to help get him home before he drank any more. He'd behaved like an idiot, likely even more so than what he actually remembered, but Jennifer had never held it against him and had accepted his apology the next time they'd met.

"Hey Jennifer, it's Danny Fitzpatrick," he said, picking up the phone.

"Hey Danny. I was hoping you'd take my call."

"What's up?"

"I think you're going to want to come over here to the station."

"Why's that?"

"I just got a really strange letter that I think is connected to the fire at the baseball game."

Danny's stomach tightened. "A letter, huh? I have a feeling I know what it says."

"I've hardly touched it. I've got it here on my desk and I thought you guys would want to come get it."

"We do. And we'll be there shortly."

**\*\*\*\***

# Chapter 15

Tessa and Danny headed to the home of Max Fugate's parents while the forensics team investigated the letter that had been sent to Jennifer Higgins.

They drove up to a tidy ranch home on Chestnut Street and pulled into the driveway next to a Toyota Corolla.

"I wonder if this is the Fugate's car or if someone else is here," Danny said as he got out of Tessa's Subaru.

"Maybe it's their daughter," Tessa said. "I hope it is. Hope they have someone here with them for support."

"Yeah," Danny said. "Might be easier for us to talk to the sister too. I didn't check on the ages of the parents but they have to be in bad shape. What a nightmare for these people."

Tessa nodded and walked to the porch where she knocked on the Fugate's front door. She and Danny both flashed their badges at a middle-aged woman who answered the knock.

Danny introduced himself and Tessa as homicide detectives as the woman opened the door to let them inside.

"I'm Cassie Jenkins," she said. "Max is…" she paused and cleared her throat. "Max was my brother."

"We're very sorry for your loss," Tessa said. "Could we talk to you a bit about your brother? We're trying to learn more about him so we can figure out who might have done this to him."

Tears fell from Cassie's eyes and dropped on the beige carpet at her feet. "We've tried to hold out hope that Max would turn up," she said. "We kept thinking there was just some terrible misunderstanding and we'd hear from Max any day now. But even though I knew it wasn't realistic to think he was still alive no matter how much we hoped he was, I never could have imagined anything like this. Not even in my worst nightmares."

"It was a terrible thing," Danny said. "We truly are sorry."

Cassie grabbed a tissue from her pocket and wiped tears from her face. "Do you need to talk to my parents? They're both upstairs lying down. After the officers came to tell us Max was dead they just couldn't...." Cassie's words dissolved into tears.

Tessa put her hand on the crying woman's arm. "It's okay. We don't need to disturb them just now. If we could talk to you that would help us a great deal."

Cassie nodded and ushered the two detectives into the dining room. She motioned for them to join her at the mahogany table at the room's center.

"Of course," she said. "Whatever I can help you with, just let me know."

"What can you tell us about your brother?" Danny asked. "We know he worked at the hospital."

"Right. He was a surgeon. Max wanted to be a doctor from the time we were kids. He loved that game Operation. I think he was the only kid who ever took it seriously. He would actually get mad if he touched the sides and caused the buzzer to go off."

Tessa smiled. "How long had he been at Fairbanks General?"

"Since he was in medical school. Max never had any interest in living anywhere but Fairbanks. He loved it here."

"Were the two of you close?"

"Yes," Cassie said, her voice cracking. "Very."

"Had Max mentioned any problems he was having to you recently? Anyone he may have had some sort of altercation or disagreement with?"

"No. Max was generally easy-going. He wouldn't tolerate any nonsense at work but otherwise he was never interested in confrontation."

"What about relationship problems? Did he have a girlfriend?"

Cassie chuckled. "No, no girlfriend. Not since he took Jocelyn Dominick to his 8th grade dance. But he did have a new boyfriend. Max was gay."

Danny immediately flashed back to the call from Nick Torrance's partner. "Was he out?" he asked.

"Yeah. Since college. Everyone knew Max was gay."

"Had anyone ever given him trouble about it? Maybe at the hospital?"

"There are always idiots around who make snide remarks. Max learned to ignore that kind of crap a long time ago. But it was never an issue as far as his job went. He is…was a really good surgeon so no one ever gave him any grief about his personal life. It's not as if the administrators would have allowed it anyway, not in this day and age. But Max was well thought of at the hospital."

"You mentioned a new boyfriend," Tessa said. "What can you tell us about him?"

"Not much. They weren't together long before Max…" Cassie blew her nose and wiped more tears from her eyes. "His name is Kris Anderson. He's a paramedic. Max and I only had one conversation about him. He said he really liked him but wasn't sure if Kris liked baseball or not. Max joked that it would be a deal-breaker if he didn't."

"So your brother was a baseball fan?"

"Big time. He followed the Mariners and loved watching the Goldpanners in the summer. Max was a good athlete. He played baseball himself all through school and he loved running now."

"He was a fit guy?"

Cassie nodded. "Yeah. He was kind of vain about being in shape to be honest," she said with a slight smile.

"What about previous boyfriends? Relationships gone bad?" Tessa asked.

"He dated Michael Stevens for years but it didn't really end badly. Mike was a surgeon too and took a job in San Diego after his residency. Max didn't want to go with him. It was an amicable split though as far as I know." Cassie let out a deep breath and struggled to keep her voice even. "Honestly, my brother was a happy guy. He didn't have a lot of drama in his life. I can't imagine anyone he's ever known doing something like this."

Cassie clutched her arms around her stomach and dissolved into another round of tears. "I'm sorry," she said. "I just don't know what to tell you."

Danny glanced at Tessa as he reached out and covered Cassie's hands with his own. "Nothing to apologize for, Cassie. You've been very helpful. I'm so sorry again about your brother."

Cassie nodded and continued to cry.

The two detectives got up from their chairs and left their business cards on the table.

"We'll leave you alone now," Tessa said. "Please give your parents our condolences. We'll be back to talk to them another time."

"And if you think of anything new that you think may help, give either one of us a call," Danny said. "We'll show ourselves out."

As they left the house and walked back to Tessa's car, Danny cursed the day he'd ever decided to become a cop. Of course, it was the only thing he'd ever planned to be, much like Max Fugate had apparently always wanted to be a surgeon. If Danny had understood the strain of dealing with people who were suffering horrific losses he would have followed another path. Or perhaps it was just since he lost his beloved Caroline that he felt this way. Now each visit with a grieving loved one brought his wife's murder back to his mind in crystal clarity. He knew all too well about the gaping hole that was now in the Fugate's lives.

"So either the sister wasn't nearly as close to her brother as she thought or this killer isn't anyone who knew Max," Tessa said. "I'm thinking the latter."

"Yeah," Danny said, sliding into the passenger seat. "We need to check out that Kris guy though. See if he knows anything the family may not have been aware of." He grabbed his tablet and brought up the browser. "I'll find out what station he works out of. With luck we can catch him at work."

Tessa nodded and backed out of the Fugate's driveway. Cassie Fugate stood at the window and watched the detectives leave. When they had, she let the curtain fall back over the window and collapsed into a sobbing heap on the floor of her parents' living room.

****

# Chapter 16

"Well here we are again, detectives," Jack Meyer said, sitting in his chair at the head of the conference room table. "I hope we have more going for us by now."

"Saw your press conference, boss," Danny said. "You were born to be on television."

"Fuck off, Fitzpatrick. I don't need your smart mouth today. Or any day for that matter but especially not today." He waited for Tessa and Danny to take their seats. "What do you know about Max Fugate?"

"He was gay," Tessa said.

Jack raised his eyebrows. "Like Torrance," he said. "Maybe this is the link we've been looking for. What else?"

"He loved his job at the hospital," Danny said. "Loved living in Fairbanks and never considered moving anywhere else. He was close to his family and had a new boyfriend named Kris Anderson who works as a paramedic over at the Crest Street station. We just came from talking to him but he couldn't tell us anything more than what Fugate's sister already had. We checked in with his colleagues at the hospital too. Everyone says the same thing. Fugate was a nice mild-mannered guy and a great surgeon. Also a good athlete who prided himself on being fit."

"You mentioned Torrance looked fit when you saw him running before the fire."

Danny nodded. "He did. Ran like an athlete. So they were both gay and they were both athletes. That about sums up what we know as far as any link between the two of them."

"I think the gay link is the one worth pursuing," Tessa said. "Have there been any other attacks on gays recently? Anti-gay activist meetings maybe?"

Jack shook his head. "Not that I've heard about."

"Has there been any more from Jennifer Higgins about the letter?"

"No. There's nothing on that letter that can help us. She and her boss have agreed to keep it out of the news for now. But they'll be off and running with our two victims starting tonight. In fact they've already got it all over their site."

"Well we weren't going to be able to keep it hidden forever. The exposure might be a good thing anyway. Maybe someone who knows something about one or both of them will see the story and contact us with something that could help us out," Danny said.

"Why don't you two try to see what you can find out about anti-gay groups in the city?" Jack said. "He glanced at the clock on the wall behind his two detectives. "Christ, this has been a long day. That can wait. Go home and get some rest."

"Where are we with the cause of the fires, sir?" Danny asked.

"Rizzo is going over everything again with a fine-toothed comb. He can't find shit and still doesn't know how the fire at the game started or what may have been used to set Max Fugate on fire."

"You know he's ready to kill himself, having all this happen right before he's set to retire," Tessa said.

"I know he is and I don't give a shit. He's not retired yet and he needs to find something for us to work with."

"It might not be his fault, sir," Danny said. "Maybe whoever is doing this has some way of starting fires we don't know about yet."

"What is that supposed to mean? You think somebody invented a new way to start a fire?"

"Could be."

"Don't go buying trouble, Fitzpatrick. You don't think we have enough already? I don't want to hear any of your whacked out theories." He held up his hand to silence Danny before he could speak. "And yes I'm aware that your theories turned out to be right up in the Arctic. We'll all aware. But that doesn't mean you can pull nonsense out of your ass now." Jack shook his head. "A new way to start a fire that nobody's ever heard of? Are you serious with this shit?"

"Just an idea," Danny said. "We can't find any traditional cause so...."

"So Rizzo will keep working on it and he'll find a cause soon enough. You two please, just go home and get some rest. You're booked on a flight to Anchorage in the morning so you can meet with Nick Torrance's partner. Maybe for once we'll get lucky and this guy can give us the magic link between Torrance and Fugate. But odds are it's just going to be yet another shitty day so you might as well get some rest while you can."

Danny gave a mock salute as he walked to the door of the conference room. "Aye, aye, Captain," he said, ducking out of the room before the wadded up ball of paper his boss threw his way could hit him in the head.

****

# Chapter 17

Jamie sat at his desk and impatiently clicked through the local news sites to read all he could about the reactions to his fires. The night shift couldn't have suited him more since he could now count on even more solitude. He could find out all he wanted to without having to worry about interruptions from his supervisor or colleagues. Everything he was finding out so far was even more entertaining than he expected.

His victims had both been identified and while the name Max Fugate was nothing new to him the identity of his second victim was intriguing. For one, he couldn't believe his luck that he'd managed to pick a visitor to the city while searching for someone to burn at the baseball game. The fact that Nick Torrance was from Anchorage would surely help confound the police more than he had dared hope. But the truly fun revelation about Nick Torrance was that he was gay.

Jamie had known Max Fugate was gay when he'd chosen him, as everyone at the hospital did, but that hadn't had anything to do with his selection. He'd merely wanted a jogger who enjoyed jogging at night while relatively few people were around. He'd started following Fugate after he'd been on the same elevator as the surgeon and heard him talking to a colleague about how much he loved jogging in Griffin Park at night. So it was merely a delightful coincidence that Nick Torrance turned out to be gay as well. Jamie loved coincidences. And this unexpected link convinced him even more that his plan was meant to be carried it out.

To his dismay, there was nothing in the news about his letters. He figured the police would keep their letter under wraps, but he had obviously guessed wrong about Jennifer Higgins. He'd been certain she would jump on the letter and use it for one of her crime features. He wondered how the police had convinced her to keep it to herself. Regardless, he was angry that he'd misjudged her, but that wasn't what he wanted to focus on now. There was too much to be happy about.

The police were sure to jump on the gay connection between his two victims. Jamie tried to imagine their conversations about the issue and chuckled a bit as he thought of the various detectives and investigators he had seen at the baseball game. He remembered the clueless cop who had questioned him and asked if he'd noticed anything suspicious at the park before the fire started.

He imagined that cop and his colleagues wondering if Jamie was an anti-gay zealot out to spread his message that homosexuality was a sin. Jamie could have some fun with this. The opportunity was too good to pass up.

****

# Chapter 18

It only took an hour to fly from Fairbanks to Anchorage, but even that short round-trip flight felt like a waste of two hours to Danny. He and Tessa had met with Andrew Cushings and discussed Nick Torrance but found absolutely nothing to link the man to Max Fugate, an outcome which surprised neither of them. They also found nothing in Torrance's present or past to suggest he had any enemies willing to burn him alive.

"I don't think our guy even knew Torrance," Danny said as he cracked his window to blow out smoke from his newly-lit cigarette. A blast of the steamy hot air outside the car greeted him immediately. He hated opening the window when he had the air conditioning on full-blast, but he knew Tessa hated the cigarette smoke. She wouldn't let him smoke in her car and he actually felt guilty about smoking now while she was in his, but after the irritation of the airport he needed a cigarette.

"I don't think so either," Tessa said, wrinkling her nose. "Why the hell did you have to take up smoking just when you became my partner?"

"I actually took it back up before I became your partner. You're the one who kept saying I needed to cut back on my drinking. And I did. But I need some kind of vice. Come on."

"If you quit smoking once before you can do it again."

"I quit because Caroline hated it and I wanted to marry her more than I wanted to keep smoking." Danny inhaled a long drag from the cigarette and blew the smoke out the window. "But she's not around to care anymore, is she?"

"She'd be disappointed if she was, I'm sure."

"I can't worry all that much about disappointing dead people. Let's get back to Torrance," Danny said. "You know if there's one thing I hate talking about it's Caroline."

Tessa thought to herself that as far as she could tell there were plenty of things Danny hated talking about beyond his murdered wife, including everything about his previous life in Chicago. Not to mention his near murder at the hands of Aleksei Nechayev. And Nechayev himself, for that matter. Danny had consistently clammed up at even the mention of his name ever since his rescue from Nechayev's Arctic house of horrors.

"Earth to Tessa."

Tessa heard her partner's voice and turned to look at him. "Sorry. I was just lost in thought for a minute I guess."

"What were you thinking about?"

"How Nick Torrance was a victim of colossal bad luck. This is the worst case of being in the wrong place at the wrong time I've ever seen," Tessa said, lying.

"Yeah, I agree there." Danny paused as he waited for the red light in front of him to turn green. "You think the killer knew Max Fugate?"

"Possible. I wouldn't be surprised. You?"

"My gut tells me he did," Danny said. "But I have nothing but my gut to back that up. I just feel like he started with someone he knew and was watching. Then he moved on to a random stranger for his big coming out party."

"I have the same feeling."

"So what now?" Danny asked.

"There's still the gay link."

"Yeah." Danny glanced at the clock on his dashboard. In spite of what felt like days in the airport, it was still only 2:00 in the afternoon. "You want to go check out that reverend with the church that has its members standing on street corners carrying signs about gays burning in hell? What's his name again?

"Richard Phillips."

"Right. From all I read he's a real fire and brimstone kind of guy and he hates gays above all else. Why don't we run by his church and see if he's available to chat with us?"

"I guess so. But this whole line of thinking doesn't ring true to me."

"Honestly I don't disagree with you. It's shoddy police work and we're grasping at a very thin straw."

"If we're operating on the assumption that Nick Torrance was a stranger to our killer then how would he have known the man was gay? It doesn't add up."

"It doesn't. But maybe we're wrong that Torrance was a stranger. And besides, we don't have anything else, do we?"

Tessa shrugged. "True enough. You know where the church is?"

"I know it's on Merrill Street. But if you're asking if I know how to get there I know you're being a smartass."

Tessa laughed. "I admit it, I am. But I think you should know your way around our city better by now."

"Why when I've got your as my personal GPS? Tell me where to go. And I don't mean hell."

Tessa chuckled again and gestured towards the windshield. "Turn left at the light," she said. "It's only about ten minutes from here."

"Great. I can't wait to meet the Reverend Phillips."

****

# Chapter 19

The Reverend Richard Phillips slumped in his chair at his New Church of God office and groaned at the stack of paperwork in front of him on his desk. Getting a new church up and running was a time-consuming endeavor and he longed for enough funding to hire an assistant. But that wasn't going to happen for quite a while at this rate, so for now he needed to keep trudging along himself. At least he had a volunteer willing to work as his secretary. He wondered how long Linda would be willing to do that but quickly pushed the thought from his mind. No need to borrow trouble.

He'd left Seward back in March and decided to move his church here to Fairbanks instead. He wanted to minister in a bigger city and the frontier atmosphere of Fairbanks appealed to him. It felt like the last stop in civilization before the long trek to the Arctic. His goal was the same as it has always been. He wanted to improve upon that civilization and convert others to his cause.

Phillips had come of age during the era of Jerry Falwell and the Moral Majority and had been inspired by the melding of religion and politics during the Reagan years. He believed strongly that the country had lost its way in the decades since and that religion needed a more prominent voice in politics. While he did not condone violence and felt a policy of civil disobedience was the best way to achieve his goals, he also didn't believe in rolling over and letting what he saw as moral decay take a stronger hold in the country. Or at least not in his beloved home state of Alaska.

He had moved to Fairbanks with the express purpose of growing his church and agitating for the cause of religious liberty in the face of the homosexual agenda. He wasn't about to sit still while the gays allowed their perverse lifestyle to take over Christian society. He'd had some success at advancing his cause in the months since he'd moved here, but he knew he still had a long road ahead of him. No rest for the righteous was his motto.

One thing Phillips hadn't planned on when he'd moved to Fairbanks was being confronted with the worst heat he'd ever experienced. He wondered how those in the lower 48 handled these types of temperatures every year. He grabbed a handkerchief from his pocket and mopped his brow before settling back down to work. Unfortunately, he didn't have more than a minute to work before he was interrupted.

"Reverend? There are two police detectives here to see you."

Phillips looked up from his paperwork to see Linda standing at the door of his office.

"Police detectives? What do they want?"

"I don't know. They just said they'd like to talk to you."

"Send them in then," he said with a scowl. He didn't have time for this. "Thank you, Linda."

"Reverend? I'm Detective Tessa Washington and this is my partner Danny Fitzpatrick. Thanks for meeting with us."

Phillips got up from his chair and walked to the door where the petite woman stood with her tall partner. He extended his hand to both of them and shook hands politely.

"I doubt I had much of a choice. But I certainly don't mind." He gestured for both Danny and Tessa to take the seats across from his desk. "Please, make yourselves comfortable."

Phillips returned to his own chair. "What can I help you with?"

"We're investigating two crimes," Danny answered. "Homicides, actually." He paused and waited for Phillips' reaction to the word. He knew he'd get one.

"Homicides? Goodness, I don't know what I could help you with on something like that. Has something happened to our church members?"

"No, nothing like that," Danny said. "At least we have no reason to believe they were members of your church and every reason to believe they weren't."

"I'm afraid I don't understand."

"The two men murdered were both gay, Reverend," Tessa said.

Phillips sat back in his chair. "Oh. Well I'm sorry to hear that but again I don't see how I could help you."

"You preach a great deal about gays, don't you?" Danny asked.

"I do. But I certainly don't preach violence."

"You've talked a lot about gays burning in hell though, haven't you?"

"Yes, I have. That's what I believe."

"Do you think any of your preaching might drive someone to get things moving here on earth? Maybe someone who doesn't think we need to wait for hell. Have you ever thought about that yourself?"

"I don't have any idea what you're talking about."

"You heard about the fire at the baseball game I'm sure," Tessa said, taking over the questioning.

"I did, yes." Phillips paused. "Wait a minute, are you talking about the man who was killed there?"

"The man who was burned alive, yes we are."

"Dear God. Do you think I had something to do with that?"

"Well we've just noticed that you're very new to our city," Danny said. "And your entire message seems to be wrapped up in anti-gay rhetoric that regularly employs the fires of hell. So we can't help but find it a little strange when two gay men turn up burned alive not long after you set up shop here."

Phillips grabbed his handkerchief and mopped his brow as the color drained from his beefy red face. He muttered a prayer and put the handkerchief back in his pocket.

"I'd never condone such atrocities."

"But you preach about the fires of hell on a regular basis."

"Hell is God's punishment, not mine. It's not for us here on earth to inflict his punishments. We can only try to preach the word so that as many as possible are spared."

"But what if they don't agree with your word? What then?" Danny asked.

"Then they answer to God. Not to me." Phillips ran his hand through his thinning brown hair. "Listen, I have never condoned violence."

"I don't think that's entirely true, Reverend," Tessa said. "According to one of your sermons on your own website here, you've likened God's destruction of Canaan for its wickedness to the need to fight against homosexuality today."

"I've warned that we can't allow our own society to descend into wickedness or we could face the same fate. I didn't suggest we ourselves should destroy it or the people in it. That will be God's work as he sees fit."

"Still, you can see how this kind of rhetoric might get people stirred up, can't you?" Danny asked.

"I don't consider it rhetoric. I consider it preaching the word of God."

"Fair enough," Danny said. "But we'd like to have a look at your church members and employees. See if anyone has anything in their past that might indicate they could decide to take your warnings into their own hands."

"You're welcome to look at whatever you like. We don't have any employees though. Linda is a volunteer and she is all the help I have. We're so new we don't have a membership directory put together yet. And people aren't required to join the church to come to our services. We welcome anyone who wants to come in."

"How about donors? Any big donations that have helped you get off the ground?" Danny asked.

"Not really anything that stands out. But Linda can show you a list of our donors and receipts for the donations we've received."

"That would be great," Tessa said as she stood up from her chair. "I do appreciate your time and your honesty in talking with us."

Phillips followed her lead and stood up himself. "As I said I'm glad to help. I don't have anything to hide here."

The last to leave his chair, Danny followed Tessa and the reverend out of his office and into the main lobby of the church. He tended to believe Phillips and, as he'd told Tessa, didn't really think he or his church had anything to do with these crimes. He thought this whole exercise was a waste of time and his instincts told him that it wasn't bringing him any closer to catching their fire-starting murderer. He thought of the letter that had been sent to the police and to the media and his stomach clenched. He only hoped they'd find something substantial before the killer answered his own question and let them all know who was next.

****

# Chapter 20

Danny and Tessa walked back out into the blazing afternoon sun and immediately started to sweat.

"Lord have mercy," Tessa said. "I feel like I'm burning in hell."

Danny chuckled. "Didn't you chastise me for being overly dramatic about the heat not too long ago?"

"Oh shut up."

Tessa opened the door to Danny's car, anxious to get back in the air conditioning. "I may start living in my car if this heat doesn't let up. I don't even know if I've ever used the AC before. Now I don't want to get out of it."

Squinting in the sun, Danny glanced across the street at a woman standing next to a Channel 10 news van.

"Isn't that Jennifer?" he asked, shielding his eyes with his hand.

Tessa turned in the direction of his gaze. "It is. What is she doing? Following us?"

Danny left the car and strode across the street. He repeated Tessa's question.

"Are you following us, Jennifer?"

"Fancy meeting you here, Danny. Are you considering joining the church?"

"Spare me the cute. What are you doing here?"

"I'm following up on a lead," Jennifer said.

"What lead?" Tessa asked.

"I'm not interested in telling you my sources. But I will say it doesn't take ferreting out a source to follow your nose and find someone in this town who might have been interested in targeting gay men and burning them alive."

"Aren't you being a little dramatic?" Danny asked.

"You're here too, aren't you? I could ask you the same."

"Jennifer, leave this alone. We're working our case, period. This isn't a news story," Danny said.

"I think that's for my producer and me to decide."

Danny felt a flash of anger. "Dammit…"

"Danny, let it go," Tessa said, putting her hand on his arm. "Jennifer's right. If she thinks there's a story here that's her business. We've got a lot of work to do."

Reluctantly, Danny followed Tessa back across the street and got into his car. Jennifer waited for them to back out of their spot and drive away before turning to her cameraman and preparing to record an introduction to her story.

**\*\*\*\***

# Chapter 21

Jamie tightened his hood closer around his face and pulled on gloves as he walked towards the New Church of God in search of the Reverend Richard Phillips. The heat of the evening made him uncomfortable in this attire, but he knew there were plenty of surveillance cameras on the street and making sure he couldn't be recognized was much more important than his comfort, or lack thereof.

He got to the church and was both pleased and unsurprised to find the door open in spite of the fact that it was nearly 11:00 at night. The fact that churches had a habit of wanting to be welcoming to those in need regardless of the time made his life a great deal easier. Or more accurately, it made his life easier for the next hour or so. Excitement over this unplanned phase of his project had his body coursing with adrenalin and he didn't have the patience to deal with trying to force his way into the building. He kept his face down and out of the view of cameras and closed the door of the church quietly behind him.

While the sun was still high in the sky and lighting up the street outside, the church was dim and poorly lit thanks to heavy curtains on the windows. Jamie knew very well that his whole plan may have to be aborted if Reverend Phillips was not at the church or if he was not here alone. But Jamie had already decided it would be easy enough to get out of that without arousing suspicion. He'd act like a depressed junkie who was finally ready to accept the Lord and the church people would eat it up. Jamie hoped it wouldn't come to that, but he was ready if it did.

He could see a light on in a room at the end of the hallway and figured it was a good bet that he could find Phillips there. He walked to the room and knocked on the open doorway. He could barely keep himself from smiling when he saw Phillips alone in the room. The reverend looked up from his stack of papers at the sound of Jamie's knock.

"Reverend Phillips?" Jamie asked.

"Yes," the man said, his face trying to hide his obvious alarm as he took in the young man wearing a hoodie and gloves in spite of the ongoing heat wave. "Can I help you with something? The church is closed right now."

"But your door was open."

Phillips cursed Linda under his breath. He knew he couldn't expect too much from a volunteer, but was it too much to ask for her to remember to lock the door?

"If you need help we're available to help you," he said, forcing his voice to stay calm. "Are you in trouble?"

"No, I'm not. But I'm afraid you are."

Phillips put down the papers he was holding. He tried to reach in his drawer for the revolver he always kept there without drawing the attention of the strange young man standing in front of him.

"What do you mean by that?" he asked. "Are you here to rob me? If so you're welcome to anything we have in the safe."

"I don't want your money. And I want you to understand that this isn't personal. I don't have any problem with you or your work."

"What isn't personal?"

Phillips' hand reached the drawer and he said more silent curses when he found it locked. He couldn't be too angry at Linda for forgetting to lock the front door. He had forgotten to unlock his own drawer when he'd arrived that morning.

"What I'm about to do. Honestly, you're just a victim of bad luck. I had no intention of coming after you until I saw the story on the news. Do you know Jennifer Higgins?"

"The woman on the news?"

"Right. She did a story on you tonight. She reported on the fact that the cops are treating you as a suspect in the fire murders."

"But I'm not a suspect. I talked to the police earlier today. I had nothing to do with those murders."

"Oh, I know you didn't. And honestly, I think the cops are idiots for running with the connection they did. It was just a coincidence that both of those men were gay."

Phillips stood up in his chair and put his hands firmly on his desk to keep them from trembling.

"How do you know it was just a coincidence?" he asked.

"You could say I'm an expert on their deaths. I'm the expert if you get right down to it."

Phillips gripped the desk more tightly and tried to mask his fear by speaking in the sternest voice he could muster.

"I'm going to need you to leave, young man. As I told you, the church is closed."

"Right but as I told you, your door was open. And you're just what I need to send a message to those idiots you spoke with today."

"A message? What are you talking about?"

Jamie fixed his eyes on Phillips with a cold and bloodless gaze.

"Like I said Reverend, this isn't personal."

"Why do you keep saying that? What isn't personal?"

Jamie ignored the questions. "YA zaklykayu BEELZEBUTH~, LUCIFER~," he said, his eyes boring into Phillips. "MADILON…"

"What are you saying?" Phillips asked.

"SOLYMO~, SAROY ~, Vizyt!"

"What are you saying?!" Phillips yelled. He felt heat coming from his hands and looked down to see tendrils of smoke rising from them. "What's happening?"

Jamie's eyes rolled back into his head. "Pozhezha!" he yelled. "Spalyuvaty!"

Phillips fell back in his chair as flames erupted from his hands. "Stop," he screamed, trying to put out the flames as they began to travel up his arms. "Stop!"

Jamie ignored the man's shrill cries for help. "Pozhezha!"

The flames spread to Phillips' chest and quickly engulfed his torso as they moved down towards his legs. "Help me!" he screamed. "Someone help me!"

Jamie's voice thundered over his screams. "Spalyuvaty!" he yelled.

Jamie opened his eyes and stared at Phillips' burning body, now barely visible through the flames. He smiled and continued his chant.

"Spalyuvaty," he said in a whisper. "Burn."

The flames extinguished any sound or sign of life from Phillips and moved on to engulf his chair. Jamie followed the fire with his eyes

79

as it devoured the leather. He didn't want to fire to spread any further. This was perfect as it was.

"Stiy," he said. "Stop."

As the flames died around Phillips' body, Jamie breathed in the smell of the burning flesh that permeated the room. Satisfied, he walked back down the hallway he had come down just a few minutes earlier. He left the church and walked out into the still blazing midnight sun.

# Chapter 22

Danny immediately covered his mouth and nose with his hand as he entered Reverend Phillips' office. He'd been to more homicide scenes than he could count and thought he had become immune to the smell but the stench in this room was like nothing he'd ever encountered.

"What the hell happened here?" he asked.

A uniformed officer with a dab of Vicks vapor rub under his nose turned towards Danny and stepped aside so Danny could get an unobstructed view of what remained of Phillips.

"The church secretary found him like this when she came in to open up the church."

"God almighty," Danny said.

"Oh my Lord," Tessa said as she walked into the room behind him.

Jack Meyer was the last to enter the room. "Goddammit, son of a bitch."

The three stared silently at the grisly scene in front of them as if mesmerized by the carnage. The uniformed officer broke the silence and held out a container.

"You guys want some Vicks? The smell is unbelievable."

Danny grabbed the container and smeared the rub under his nose before passing it to his colleagues. "Thanks," he said. "Are the ME's on their way?" he asked.

The officer nodded his head yes. "We talked with the secretary but she couldn't tell us much. She's hysterical, as you'd expect. My partner's trying to help her get calmed down now."

"What'd she tell you?" Tessa asked.

"Just that she went home last night around 7:00 and the reverend said he planned to stay at the church and work late. He was working on paperwork here at his desk when she said goodnight to him. She didn't notice anything strange before she left. She said the only thing unusual that went on yesterday was you guys coming to talk to Phillips."

Danny frowned. "So I guess this was the answer to who was next."

"No, I don't think this was a planned target for him. He's playing with us," Tessa said. "He wants to send the message that the first two victims were gay had nothing to do with why he chose them."

Jack glanced around the room and up at the ceiling, letting out an audible sigh of relief when he saw a security camera pointed at the desk. "Looks like the preacher had a camera installed. Please somebody tell me it was working."

"The secretary said he always had it running since he kept the church safe in here," the uniformed officer said. "The monitor is out by her desk."

The ME's and an increasingly beleaguered Anthony Rizzo entered the room and immediately took over the scene to begin their investigations. Danny, Tessa and Jack took the opportunity to go back to the front of the church and review the security camera footage.

Danny sat down at Linda's desk while Jack and Tessa pulled up chairs next to him. He grabbed the mouse and brought up the video stream on the computer.

"The secretary said she left around seven last night. Let's start there and skim through it," Jack said.

Danny chose the time to start the stream and set it to play at three times the normal speed. Jack and Tessa pulled their chairs closer to the monitor as the three watched the footage of Phillips' office before it had become an inferno.

"It makes me feel so strange to see those chairs we were sitting in just yesterday," Tessa said. "I feel like we got this man killed. We both knew this was a shoddy lead. We never should have questioned the reverend."

Danny frowned. "I wish we hadn't but how could we have predicted this for Christ's sake? And I don't think Jennifer Higgins is blameless either. She never should have reported on our suspicions."

"Both of you shut up," Jack said. "No one is responsible for this except the son of a bitch who keeps setting these fires. Now let's just

82

hope to God he shows up on this camera and we can haul his sorry ass in."

The three watched in frustration as they watched Reverend Phillips writing notes and pushing papers around his desk. At one point, he appeared to consult a ledger and at another time he opened his Bible and read through several pages. Danny felt his fingers growing itchy to increase the fast-forward, but knew he had to be patient.

After what felt like an eternity, their patience was finally rewarded. A slender male figure wearing jeans and a hooded sweatshirt entered the screen and faced Phillips' desk.

Danny froze the screen. "There he is," he said. "The son of a bitch has his hood up so tightly around his head we can't see anything."

"And he's wearing gloves," Tessa said. "He made sure we wouldn't even be able to see what color his skin is."

"Keep it going," Jack said. "He might turn around and look right at us."

The three watched as Phillips and the man appeared to be having a conversation. It was obvious to anyone watching that Phillips was ill at ease.

"Dammit, why can't these things have sound?" Jack asked.

Phillips stood up and grabbed his desk as he stared at the man in the hoodie. Within seconds, the three cops' eyes widened in horror as flames began to shoot out of the man's hands.

"This is where it starts," Danny said. "How'd he do it?"

No one answered as they continued to watch in horror.

"Oh that poor man," Tessa whispered as the flames engulfed Phillips' body and he collapsed back in his chair. The man in the hoodie remained still as he stared at the burning man in front of him.

The fire began to lick the leather of the chair and appeared ready to take over the desk and move on to the rest of the room when it suddenly started to die out as quickly as it had started. The flames became smaller and began to fold into themselves. Within seconds, there was nothing but smoke emanating from the dead man and his burned chair.

After the fire was extinguished, the man in the hoodie calmly turned and walked out of the room, never once looking up at the camera. He kept his face to the floor and completely out of view.

"How did he do that?" Danny asked again. "How could he have started that fire?"

"And how did he stop it?" Jack asked. "Why didn't the flames take over the whole room?"

No one had an answer to any of the questions.

"We don't know that he started it," Tessa said. "He was just standing there."

"Well how the hell else do you think it started?" Danny asked.

"I have no idea. And neither do you. So don't get smart with me, Danny."

Danny scowled and rewound the footage to watch the scene again. Watching Phillips stand up and grab his desk made his stomach turn now that he knew exactly what was coming next. He could feel the bile rising in his throat.

"I don't know if I can watch this again," Tessa said.

She didn't move as all three watched the horror unfold once again on the screen in front of them.

"He doesn't even move his hands to throw something that could have started the fire," Jack said. "He's just standing there. It's like he's telekinetic for Christ's sake and he just did it with his mind."

"Telekinetic people don't start fires with their minds."

"Sure they do," Jack said. "I've seen Carrie. She burned the whole damn gym down."

"I've seen Carrie too. She set the fire by spraying the fire hose around the gym. The water hit an electrical apparatus and sparked the blaze." Danny ignored the stares of his colleagues. "What? I've seen the movie a bunch of times, okay? Back to the point, telekinesis means moving something with your mind. It doesn't mean setting fires."

"What are you, Fitzpatrick? Some kind of paranormal expert?"

Danny didn't answer and continued to stare at the screen, now showing only the smoldering remains of the reverend.

"I wasn't really suggesting the asshole used telekinesis anyway." Jack said.

"Well he used something," Tessa said. "I'm gonna go talk to Antony and see what he's found out there."

"I'm going out on a limb and saying he won't have found anything." Danny said. He ignored the irritated stare Tessa shot his way before she left the room.

"I'm going with her," Jack said. "I want to talk to the secretary and the MEs."

"We also need to check security cameras outside on the street," Danny said. "I'll start on that."

"Good," Jack said, getting up from his chair.

Danny didn't move his eyes from the monitor as his boss left the room. He fumbled in his pocket for a cigarette. Lighting it, he inhaled deeply and let the smoke slowly leave his mouth. He figured no one was going to notice the smell of a cigarette in this building today.

Sitting back in his chair, Danny rewound the footage and once again watched the unknown assailant burn Richard Phillips alive.

\*\*\*\*

# Chapter 23
## Sydney, Australia

Aleksei Nechayev sipped his coffee as he booted up his laptop and connected to the Koala Café's free wireless. This café had always been one of his favorites in Australia, primarily because it was open around the clock, which meant it was open during his prime hours in the middle of the night.

He smiled at his waitress who was now serving a group of college students who had come to the café for breakfast after a marathon night of partying. The waitress was quite pretty and he had grown fond of her during this trip to Sydney. She never questioned why he only appeared in the middle of the night and instead always offered him a trusting smile. She was too trusting, of course, but that only made her more appealing to him. Perhaps before he left the city he'd show her how wrong she had been to trust him.

As he always did when he got online, Aleksei went straight to the Alaska news websites. He missed his Arctic home and still couldn't believe that when the Southern hemisphere winter ended he wouldn't be returning to it this year.

He was already feeling at loose ends, especially since Katya, the girl he had chosen as his permanent companion, had abandoned him last month when he'd first brought her to Australia. She had laughed in his face and told him that he was too old and too conservative for her tastes. He had no idea where she had gone to, but she had taunted him with the knowledge that she already had her sights on a new boyfriend and couldn't wait to explore what the world had to offer with him. Wherever she was, Aleksei only hoped she would one day come to a nasty and violent end.

The inquisitive Fairbanks detective Danny Fitzpatrick had ruined the peaceful home Aleksei had maintained in the Arctic town of

Coldfoot for decades. He enjoyed checking in on the detective and, while he couldn't help but feel a strange fondness for the man he had chosen to let live, he always hoped to find him struggling with some new problem. He was tickled to see that this time he got his wish.

Aleksei grinned from ear to ear as he read about the mysterious fires that were plaguing Fairbanks while the city suffered through its worst heat wave in history. How fascinating! And by all accounts, the police, including the dear detective, had no idea who was starting the fires or even how they were doing it.

Fire was one of the few things Aleksei feared and hated as much as humans did. He still remembered the time he had been nearly burned to death by a male witch not long after he'd arrived in Alaska. He couldn't help but wonder if a supernatural force was responsible for these fires as well. Was there a witch on the loose in Fairbanks?

Since he was safe and sound on the other side of the world, Aleksei desperately hoped so. How would his favorite detective deal with a situation like that? And what of the fire starter? What was his, or her, motivation? What was the game?

His lousy winter here in Australia had suddenly taken a surprisingly lovely turn. Clearly, the summer in Fairbanks was turning out to be more horrific than anyone there could have imagined. He couldn't wait to see how it all unfolded. It was going to be such fun.

\*\*\*\*

# Chapter 24
## Fairbanks, Alaska

"There's nothing on the surveillance cameras out on the street to help us," Danny said to Tessa, who was next to him at her desk. "We see the guy walking to the church with his hood up and his gloves on. He stops to pull the hood closer around his face right as he gets to the church. The bastard didn't look up once."

"You'd think someone would have noticed him dressed so peculiarly for this heat," Tessa said. "Especially the gloves. Who walks down the street wearing gloves when it's 90 degrees?"

"The uniforms are still canvassing but so far they haven't turned up anything."

It had been 24 hours since they'd discovered the burned body of Richard Phillips and the frustrated detectives were no closer to finding out who had committed the horrific crime. Worse, the media was running with the stories of the three burnings and the city was edging closer to a full-fledged panic.

"There's something we're missing," Tessa said. "Anthony couldn't find any cause to the fire, we can't see the guy actually doing anything to start the fire on the video…" Her voice trailed off as she knew she was merely repeating words the cops had said over and over again to themselves and to each other.

Danny bit his tongue and continued watching the street surveillance footage on his computer. He was more certain than ever that he knew what they were missing. Or maybe he didn't know exactly what it was, but he knew it wasn't of this world. He knew it was something from the supernatural world whose existence Aleksei Nechayev had made all too real to him.

The ringing of the phone on his desk snapped Danny out of his trance.

"Fitzpatrick."

"Detective, there's a man on the phone who said he wants to speak with you about the fire case. He wouldn't give his name but asked for you specifically."

Danny rolled his eyes. Some nutcase, no doubt.

"Go ahead and transfer him," he said.

Danny heard the click of the call coming to his line.

"This is Detective Fitzpatrick," he said, propping the phone between his shoulder and his ear and he typed on his keyboard to bring up more surveillance footage.

"Hello, Detective."

Danny's fingers froze on his keyboard. He felt a chill wash over his body despite the boiling hot temperature in the office. He would never forget that voice. Aleksei Nechayev.

"Hello? Detective Fitzpatrick?"

Danny took the phone from his shoulder and sat up straight in his chair.

"What do you want?" he asked.

"I suppose I shouldn't have expected a friendly greeting."

Danny remained silent and noticed Tessa looking at him with a questioning expression on her face. He waved a hand as if to suggest the call was nothing and turned his back to his partner, relieved when he heard her get up from her chair and walk away from him. Still, he kept his voice low.

"I asked what you wanted. Why are you calling here?"

"I've just read about your new case that has Fairbanks buzzing. Or burning would be more accurate, wouldn't it?"

"And?"

"And I wanted to hear more about it. Who do you think is behind it? How are they doing it? Oh wait, you don't know the answer to that question, do you?"

"I'm hanging up. Don't call here again."

"Oh, come on. Don't you even want to know how I'm doing? Where I am?"

Danny paused and looked at the caller ID on his phone. The number had been blocked. "You're not here in Alaska, are you?"

"In the summer, are you kidding? With that sun I'd be burning up

# Polar Day

just like your victims. No, don't worry; I'm far away from you on the other side of the world. I'm in Sydney, Australia to be exact. The Southern hemisphere is much healthier for me this time of year."

"Okay. So I'll ask you again. What do you want?"

"You got my postcard from St. Petersburg, didn't you?"

"I did. And I sent an anonymous tip to the police that I had reason to suspect one of the most wanted murderers in the world was there in their city."

"Right, of course you did. And I imagine you'll be notifying the Sydney authorities as well. But before you do that, you might want to give it some thought. And you might want to look up an incident that happened to several St. Petersburg officers not long after you made your report. It was a terrible thing, really. A bloody mess. But Katya and I had a ball."

"You son of a bitch."

"I could say the same about you. I tried to send you a friendly greeting and you set the police on me."

"I don't have time for this. I'm working."

"I know. That's why I called. I want to talk about the case you're working on. What do you think about it? Do you think a monster is behind it? A literal one, I mean."

"You mean one like you?"

"Well, no. Trust me; my kind wouldn't be setting fires. We hate them even more than you do."

"So I've heard. Wish I'd known that when I went to Coldfoot."

"I guess you should have done better research. Luckily for me you didn't. But you still haven't answered my question."

"I have no idea who is doing it." Danny paused and bit his lip. Should he really continue this conversation? Remembering the burned body of the Reverend Phillips, he answered his own question. Maybe he could actually get something useful from Aleksei. "Do you have any ideas?" he asked. "Is that why you're calling?"

"You mean am I calling to help you? Maybe. I don't really have anything else to do. Katya left me, if you can believe that. That little bitch."

Danny couldn't suppress a smile. At least Aleksei didn't always get what he wanted.

90

Julie Flanders

"And it may interest you to know" Aleksei continued, "that I was almost killed by fire when I first came to Alaska."

"Is that right? Too bad it was 'almost.'"

He heard Aleksei's chuckle on the other end of the line.

"You still hate me, obviously," he said.

"Yes, I do," Danny answered. "Obviously."

"Regardless, I was almost burned to death by a Ukrainian who knew witchcraft. Black magic. That exists, did you know that?"

"I didn't."

"Now you do. I became a bit of an expert on it after the attempt to burn me to death didn't work. I wanted to know what I was up against if it ever happened again."

"You're an expert on witchcraft?"

"Not all of it. But fire magic is interesting to me. And wouldn't it be interesting if that's what is behind your cases there? What would you tell your colleagues? Or the media? Imagine what they'd do with a story like that."

"Yeah, just imagine it."

"Well, I merely called as a friend to offer you advice. You'd be smart to heed it. You might be able to stop this murderer in his tracks."

"And why exactly do you want to help stop a murderer? I would think you'd actually be admiring his work."

"I am. But I can't abide his methods. I told you, I hate fire. And besides, I want to see what you'll do with my advice. Will you consider this possibility at the risk of your career? How would it make you feel if your colleagues all considered you insane?"

"Believe me, that wouldn't be anything too new for me. And thanks to you, there isn't much I won't consider. I really don't need your advice."

"If you do decide you'd like to know more about fire and witchcraft, you can always call me. My cell number is 4555-55555. The country code is 61 for Australia."

"I don't want or need your number. And I'm hanging up now. Don't call me again."

Danny ended the call before Aleksei could respond. He looked down at the notepad in front of him, on which he had scribbled Aleksei's cell number. He tore the paper off the pad and stuck it in his drawer. There was no harm in writing it down. But he had no intention of ever calling it.

****

# Chapter 25

"Who was that on the phone?" Tessa asked. She walked towards Danny and sat back down at her desk.

"What? Oh, no one," Danny said. "Some nut who wanted to let me know that the fires were a sign of the apocalypse."

"Strange that he asked for you personally."

Danny shrugged. "He probably read about my exploits up in the Arctic and remembered my name from that."

"I guess so. Still nothing on the surveillance cameras?"

"No. And I've got nothing from the church donation list. There was nobody with a record or a history of trouble."

"I've been going over the hospital employee records looking for something that stands out just in case our killer did know Max Fugate. There's nothing though."

"I guess it would be too easy to find an arsonist among Max Fugate's colleagues, wouldn't it?"

Danny got up from his chair and ran his hands through his mop of thick hair. He stared out at the sun beating mercilessly down on the sidewalk and watched the pedestrians who were walking past. Would one of these people be burned next? Or was one of them the arsonist who was doing the burning?

"Do you think he'll send us another message?" he asked.

"I hope he does. Maybe it would give us something to work with."

Danny flopped back into his chair. "This is a nightmare," he said.

Tessa closed her laptop and stood up from her desk. "I've got an appointment to take Maya to the vet."

"Something wrong?"

"No, she's just due for her vaccinations. And I'm tired of looking at nothing here. I'm hoping that if I step away from it for a little while something will hit me when I come back."

"That would be nice, but I don't expect it. We've got a big old pile of nothing, period."

"I'll see you later. Call me if something breaks."

Danny nodded and turned to his own laptop. It was true, he and Tessa had nothing. Or was there something they had that neither one wanted to consider? Danny had known from the time he'd seen the shadow in front of Nick Torrance that there was something strange about this case. He'd known it when he'd watched the faceless young man on the church surveillance camera burn Richard Phillips to a crisp without moving a muscle. But now Aleksei Nechayev had said aloud what Danny never could. There was something supernatural about this case.

There was a reason none of their conventional investigative methods were yielding any results. However these fires were happening, the method wasn't of this world. It was part of something most people would never believe existed. Danny counted himself among those people who never would have believed it before he'd been forced to acknowledge the existence of the supernatural in the form of Aleksei Nechayev. Was the vampire now right about black magic? Amanda had mentioned magic when he'd told her about the chanting the kids at the baseball game heard. Maybe he should have followed up on her idea. But how could he go about doing that?

Danny clicked on his browser and glanced around the room to make sure no one was paying any attention to what he was doing. All he needed was for one of his colleagues to walk up on him and see him searching for magic shops. It would be even worse if Jack Meyer walked up on him and saw it. He'd never hear the end of it.

Convinced no one was watching him, Danny googled Fairbanks and magic. To his amazement, the city did have its own magic store called Locklear's Metaphysical Mementos. Well, it was listed as a Wiccan store, but Danny figured it was probably the same thing. Or close enough anyway. As far as he knew, wiccans cast spells. They would likely have magical ingredients. Or whatever the hell people used to cast spells.

Part of him couldn't believe he was following this train of thought. But then he remembered Aleksei staring at him with his fangs exposed. And the monster who had once been a teenager named Katie entering the room with the same fangs and the same bloodlust.

Danny browsed the online section of the store and clicked on cauldrons and amulets, rune stones and pendulums. He brought up spell ingredients such as bat's eye, dove's blood, and something called goofer's dust. Could someone use items such as these to start fires? Remembering the teens' report of hearing chanting at the baseball game prior to the fire, Danny clicked on a link for spell books. He rolled his eyes when he came upon a "spell-a-day" almanac.

Thinking he heard footsteps coming up behind it, Danny slammed his laptop shut lest anyone see what he was browsing. He glanced around and realized he had imagined the footsteps. It was nearly 8:00 and except for the night shift officers almost everyone had left the office. He scowled and grabbed his laptop from his desk as he stood up to do the same.

He could almost hear his old colleagues in Chicago laughing their asses off if they knew he was perusing a Wiccan store looking for spells to create fire. The majority of his Fairbanks colleagues already thought he was a crazy drunk. He couldn't really argue their point.

Danny walked outside and felt beads of sweat immediately gathering on his forehead. He got in his car and turned the air conditioning on full blast as he lit a cigarette and gratefully inhaled the nicotine. He couldn't let himself go off the rails with this case. Yes, he knew there was something odd about the fires. But he had come upon plenty of odd things in Chicago long before he'd ever heard the name Aleksei Nechayev. And they'd all had rational explanations.

He needed to follow Tessa's lead on this. She was right that they were simply missing a piece of the puzzle and the way to finding it was through good old-fashioned police work, not hocus pocus. Danny had solved the Nechayev case when a cold case he was working on bore striking similarities to Nechayev's last victim. That was how investigations worked sometimes. Days or weeks or even months of fruitless leads and tedious monotony until all of the sudden you connected a few dots and blew the whole thing wide open.

Danny may not know how their arsonist was setting his deadly fires but he did know that the man wasn't new to whatever game he was playing. No one was born a sophisticated criminal who was astute enough to taunt the police and media without getting caught. This guy had to have left a trail somewhere. Danny didn't need to worry about amulets or cauldrons or spells. He just needed to find that trail.

Feeling strangely invigorated, Danny pulled out of the parking lot and vowed to keep Aleksei Nechayev out of his head. He'd go home and spend the evening with Sox and watch some baseball. A night away from the case was just what he needed. He would start fresh tomorrow with the cold case arson files. He just had one stop to make before he went home.

He turned into his favorite liquor store and got out of the car. Getting Nechayev out of his mind wasn't going to be easy. Five minutes later, Danny returned to the car with a 12 pack of beer and a bottle of scotch. He needed a drink.

****

# Chapter 26

Jamie walked into his apartment and headed straight for his bedroom. He couldn't remember when he'd been so tired. He pulled off his work clothes and tossed them onto a chair, then pulled down the shades to keep the sun out and the room as dark as possible. Lighting a single candle, he fell into his bed and lay flat.

He stared at the ceiling and watched the flicker of fire from the candle dancing across it. Closing his eyes, he drew deep breaths to center his mind. While he had enjoyed his immolation of the Reverend Phillips immensely, his impulsive behavior had been a mistake. He hadn't given his body enough time to regain its strength or his mind enough time to restore his balance. Now he was paying the price.

He needed to lay low and allow his stamina to return. It wasn't as if he was in any danger of being caught before he finished his summer plans. The cops were showing themselves to be the idiots they always were. They were running around in circles and didn't have the first clue how to stop the fires that would soon destroy their city.

On one level, Jamie couldn't help but wish he had an adversary who was worthy of him. Surely one of the cops should be smart enough to actually take him on. It would make the whole experience more enjoyable.

But he knew it was just as well the police weren't up to the challenge. He didn't need any distractions or nuisances to stand in the way of Fairbanks getting what it deserved.

In a few weeks, he'd be ready to start giving his fellow Fairbanks residents more glimpses of their future. And by August, he'd burn their city to the ground.

****

# Chapter 27

*July 4, 2013*

Independence Day was traditionally a fun affair in Fairbanks and a high point of the all too short summer season. But unlike the parties held in the majority of US cities, Fairbanks' celebration did not include fireworks. Since the sun would not set until 12:30 in the morning and twilight lingered until the sun reappeared three hours later, the Fairbanks' summer skies were never dark enough to accommodate fireworks.

Instead, Fairbanks residents saved their fireworks for the winter, when darkness blanketed their city and they were lucky to see three or four hours of daylight in a 24-hour period. The city regularly set off fireworks each December 31 to help ring in another new year.

But the residents enjoyed the same picnics and parades that marked the Fourth in communities throughout the Lower 48. And in spite of the record-breaking heat that had tormented them all summer and showed no signs of ebbing as Fourth of July rolled around, they were determined to enjoy a traditional Independence Day. In Fairbanks, that meant heading to Pioneer Park.

The start of the new month had brought a sense of relief throughout the city, as nearly two weeks had passed since there had been any sign of the horrifying fires that had claimed three lives at the start of the summer. Residents were all too willing to put the fires in the past in spite of the fact that the arsonist responsible had not been found.

Many convinced themselves that the fires had been some sort of crazy fluke, bizarre coincidences that had been brought on by the unrelenting heat. The heat was an anomaly in Alaska, something most in Fairbanks had never felt, so who was to say what problems it could cause? Brush fires could have been behind the two deaths in the park, some said. Others pointed out that an air conditioner that had rarely been used could easily have overheated and started the church fire that had killed the reverend.

No matter how implausible these explanations were, frightened and tired people could convince themselves of anything when all they wanted to do was move on with their lives. Fairbanks needed to get back to normal and there was no better time than the Fourth of July for that to happen.

And so, residents beleaguered from fear and frustrated by heat headed to Pioneer Park for the annual Independence Day celebration. Pioneer Park was more than just a city park; it was also a homage to both the city's and the state of Alaska's history. Gold Rush town featured many restored buildings from Fairbanks' founding era, including the city's first church, and Pioneer Hall housed a museum featuring many artifacts from the Gold Rush years. Children loved climbing on board the SS Nenana, a sternwheeler that once sailed the Chena River. A highlight of any trip to the park was a visit to the Alaska Native village. In addition to these attractions, the park was also home to a theater and art gallery.

The park's schedule for July Fourth was packed with events, including performances by the United States Army Alaska Warrior Band and the Fairbanks Community Band, as well as gospel and folk singers from the area. The high point of the day was the kids' parade through the park. As the children waited for their chance to march in the parade, they were entertained with games, roving clowns and a booth for face painting.

A young girl barely managing to sit still while getting her face painted was the first to see the smoke coming from the Frontier Saloon in Gold Rush town. She closed her eyes tightly, hoping that when she opened them the smoke would be gone. Instead, she opened her eyes and saw flames licking the corner of the old saloon.

She turned to her father, causing the painter to brush a line of red pain beyond her face into her blond hair. The girl pointed towards the saloon and both her father and the painter followed her finger with their eyes. The painter dropped her bowl of bright yellow paint and screamed.

\*\*\*\*

# Chapter 28

*July 20, 2013*

"You think he'll hit again here?" Danny asked his partner Tessa, who was beside him as they paced the block surrounding the Carlson Center on the banks of the Chena River.

"I can't imagine he'd pass it up. This is the biggest celebration of the summer. It seems like he wouldn't be able to resist wreaking more havoc and scaring the hell out of folks."

"You mean scaring them more than he already has? It looks to me like most people were afraid to even come out for the parade today. Take the cops out of this crowd and there might be ten people here; if that."

Tessa sighed. "I don't think it's quite that bad but you're right, the crowd is nothing like it's been in the past. And that's a damn shame. Golden Days has always been a lot of fun for people here. One more big party before the summer starts slipping away from us."

The Golden Days celebration was held each year to celebrate Fairbanks' past and to commemorate the discovery of gold in a nearby creek by a man named Felix Pedro on July 22, 1902. Pedro's find set off the gold rush that led to the incorporation of the city in 1903.

The first celebration was held in 1952 and had now grown to include a street fair, comedy night, a rubber-duckie race and, the traditional highlight of the festival, the parade. It was billed as the largest in all Alaska. Filled with floats, marching bands, baton twirlers, clowns, and antique cars, the parade began at the Carlson Center and wound its way through downtown, ending up at the intersection of Noble and Airport Way. With the tagline "The Gold & The Beautiful," Golden Days was a fun-filled week giving residents the chance to celebrate the pride they felt for both their city and their state.

Danny knew Tessa was right. The arsonist, who had struck again on July 4 and burned down most of the historic Gold Rush Town in Pioneer Park, would not miss a chance to leave his mark on the cherished Golden Days celebration. He may even be disappointed that no one had been killed in his Pioneer Park fire and want to remedy that by adding to his body count today.

While the residents of Fairbanks had done their best to put on a brave face and carry on with their lives as the arsonist struck again and again over the summer, the incident at Pioneer Park had left them shaken to the core. City officials had done their best to persuade residents that all manner of precautions were being taken to insure a safe and fun Golden Days celebration, with the Fairbanks police and fire departments standing on guard and ready at all scheduled events, but it was clear from the size of the crowd gathered to watch the parade that those assurances had fallen on deaf ears. Most of Fairbanks had chosen to stay home.

"I'm actually glad it's a small crowd," Danny said. "That might make it easier for us to spot this asshole if he shows up."

"True enough."

Tessa turned to her right as the music started to play and the first band marched past the Carlson Center. The majorettes in front forced themselves to smile broadly in a failed effort to mask the fear that was evident on their faces. The two detectives scanned the sidewalks and few revelers who clapped in support of the band, but saw nothing unusual.

"I don't even know who or what to look for," Tessa said. "I don't think our guy will do us the favor of showing up with a lighted torch or a flamethrower."

"If only," Danny said.

The parade continued and both the crowd and the participants started to relax and enjoy themselves as the clowns, mini-cars and go-karts passed by and the Fairbanks high school floats made their entrance.

"Maybe he's not going to show up," Tessa said.

Before Danny could respond, a scream pierced the festive atmosphere.

"Fire!"

Danny and Tessa ran towards the sound of the scream, joined by other officers who were covering their stretch of the parade route. By now, others were yelling and pointing towards the lot of the Carlson Center, where flames were spreading among the parked cars. The fire crews on the scene immediately sprang into action, honking their horns to move the shocked and panicked parade-goers out of the way of their trucks.

"Which one of you yelled first?" Danny asked as he and Tessa ran up to a group of parade goers, some stunned into silence, others crying and sobbing hysterically.

A petite blond woman held up her hand. "I did," she said, fighting back tears. "I saw one of the cars start on fire."

"Did you see anyone by the car? Was there anyone inside?"

"No. I just glanced over there because my husband was supposed to be joining me here and I wondered if he would still be able to find a place to park. It happened so quickly. One second the car was parked there and the next it just burst into flames."

"Christ Almighty who is doing this?" a man standing next to the woman yelled. "What are you cops doing? Can't you stop this?"

"Sir, we understand you're upset," Tessa said. "We all are. But right now we need everyone to remain calm so we can talk to all of you about what you may or may not have seen. We all want this to stop."

A siren announced the arrival of another fire crew to battle the fire, which had now spread to more than a dozen cars in the lot and threatened to reach the building. Danny and Tessa looked at each other as they ushered the witnesses out of the path of the approaching truck. It was going to be another long day.

****

# Chapter 29

Jamie relaxed his yoga pose and leaned back against the bottom of his couch. He smiled as he imagined the scene at the Carlson Center right at this moment; the clueless police officers and detectives scampering around interviewing witnesses, the firefighters putting out the fire before it engulfed more cars. Even the media would be arriving en masse and fighting to secure the most advantageous position from which to report the latest fire. Jamie wished he could be there. But his imagination was a fine substitute.

He had enjoyed perfecting his skill by setting today's fire and the fire at Pioneer Park. This activity didn't require nearly as much stamina and concentration as his in-person efforts did. And he now knew he could set a fire anywhere in the city, whether he was there himself or not. Best of all, it had been fun to frighten the city's residents just as they were being lulled into a false sense of security.

In spite of the energy it took to set these fires, Jamie felt rested and he knew his full strength and power had returned. His midsummer games had been akin to the middle of a play. Now he was ready for the climax.

\*\*\*\*

# Chapter 30
*July 23, 2013*

"How about if I stand here, Bob?" Jennifer Higgins asked. "Is this okay?"

"That's fine," her cameraman Bob Spencer said. "I'm ready whenever you are."

Jennifer positioned herself in front of the closed building that had once been the New Church of God before Richard Phillips was so brutally killed less than a month earlier. The investigation into the death of Phillips, along with the deaths of Nick Torrance and Max Fugate earlier in the summer, had stalled while non-fatal fires at Pioneer Park and the Carlson Center had set the city on edge. Jennifer felt it was time to light a fire under the Fairbanks police department. Whatever was going on, the people of Fairbanks deserved to know what those getting paid to protect them were doing to find the arsonist who was terrifying the city and burning people alive.

Like many of the streets in Fairbanks, the street where the New Church of God had once stood was deserted. City residents were staying indoors as much as possible, hoping that they would at least be safe from fire inside their own homes. Jennifer could understand the sentiment. She hated coming outside now herself but she wasn't about to let some pyromaniac keep her from doing her job.

Jennifer composed her face and prepared to deliver her segment with a solemn and appropriately concerned expression. She knew the evening anchorman Jason Griffey would be introducing her when the news aired.

"Thank you and good evening, Jason," she said, staring into the camera. "Although I can't say I have much good news to report."

Bob stood in for Jason and fed her the line the anchorman would be reading that evening.

"People around Fairbanks are more worried than ever about the fire murders, Jennifer. What is the latest on the police investigation?"

Jennifer started to answer when a movement behind the cameraman distracted her. She saw the figure of a man in shadow coming up behind Bob. The figure vanished as quickly as it appeared.

"Did you hear someone behind you?" she asked.

Bob glanced around at the street behind him. "No."

"I saw someone, just for a second. I thought he was going to get in the way of our shot."

"Well there's nobody here now. Maybe you just imagined it." Bob turned his eyes towards the boiling mid-afternoon sun. "This damn sun will play tricks on anyone's eyes. Never thought I'd say this, but I can't wait for winter."

Jennifer nodded but felt a chill maneuvering up her spine. She knew she hadn't imagined anything. Someone, or something, had been there.

"She didn't imagine it," a male voice said.

Jennifer jumped and looked to her right in the direction of the voice. "Who said that? Bob?"

The cameraman shook his head. "I didn't say anything."

"Did you hear it? Hear him?"

"I did."

"Of course you heard me. I'm standing right beside you."

Jennifer took a few steps backwards. She had felt hot breath on her neck as she heard the words.

"Who are you?" she asked, her voice trembling. "Where are you?"

"I'm right here, next to you."

"Bob, what the hell is going on?"

The cameraman remained silent and stood stock still as he stared at Jennifer in disbelief. He heard the man's voice talking to her, but saw no one beside her. He looked around and couldn't see a single soul anywhere else on the sidewalk. He set his camera down on the ground so his shaking hands would not drop it.

The disembodied voice suddenly boomed across the sidewalk, causing both Bob and Jennifer to jump. "YA zaklykayu BEELZEBUTH~, LUCIFER~," the unseen man said. "MADILON…"

"What?" Jennifer asked. "What are you saying? Where are you?"

"SOLYMO~, SAROY ~, Vizyt!"

"What are you saying?!" Jennifer yelled. She felt heat coming from her feet and looked down to see flames shooting out from the toes of her shoes. "Oh my God! No, no! Bob, help!"

Jennifer stamped her feet to try to put out the flames, but the fire merely traveled up her legs and began to lick at her torso.

"Pozhezha!" the man yelled. "Spalyuvaty!"

"Bob!" Jennifer screamed.

Bob stood frozen in terror as the fire exploded around Jennifer. Finding his courage, he ran towards her, only to have the heat of the flames slam him backwards into the ground. He fumbled in his pocket for his phone and dialed 911.

"Help!" Jennifer yelled, her voice overcome with agony. "Someone help me please!"

"We need help here!" Bob yelled when a woman answered his call. "There's a fire, please help us. Please!"

"Where are you, sir?"

"The New Church of God. Jennifer's burning. Oh my God please help us!"

Bob leapt back as a flame shot out and burned his fingers. He dropped his phone in the flames, which now totally engulfed his colleague. Jennifer was no longer visible in the inferno.

He gaped in terror as the voice took on the form of a man. A shadowy figure stood there just as Jennifer had described.

"Pozhezha! Spalyuvaty!" the figure yelled.

Tears rolled down Bob's face as he watched Jennifer's body crumple to the sidewalk. She no longer screamed. He heard the man's voice again, much softer this time.

"Stiy," he said.

As quickly as it had started, the fire died down and the flames disappeared. Smoke rose from the charred corpse that just moments before had been the living and breathing Jennifer Higgins.

Bob heard the sirens of the fire department coming towards him. The shadowy figure was gone.

**\*\*\*\***

# Chapter 31

"This is Jennifer?" Danny asked as he walked up to Tessa and stared at the still smoldering shell of a person on the sidewalk.

"Yes."

The contents of Danny's stomach raced up his throat. He turned away from the corpse and forced them back down. A veteran homicide detective didn't vomit at a crime scene no matter how grisly it was. But then, he usually didn't know the victims he found at such scenes. He heard his boss coming up behind him. Uncharacteristically silent, Jack couldn't manage a one-liner or even a rant consisting of his customary expletives. The scene left him speechless.

Tessa gestured toward a thin black man sitting against the wall of the New Life Church of God. His skin was ashen and his teeth chattered as if he was frozen in spite of the fact that the boiling sun had brought the temperature to a record 95 degrees. A paramedic squatted beside the man and took his blood pressure.

"That's Jennifer's cameraman Robert Spencer," Tessa said. "He said they came here to film a bit for a piece she was putting together on the fires and our stalled investigation. I couldn't get much out of him. The poor man is in shock."

The paramedic removed the blood pressure cuff from Spencer's arm and mouthed "okay" to the detectives as he stood up and walked away from the witness. Danny ventured over and sat down next to Spencer against the wall.

"Mr. Spencer? I'm Detective Danny Fitzpatrick."

"I know who you are. You found those women in the Arctic."

"My fame precedes me. I was also a friend of Jennifer's. Did you two work together long?"

"Long enough. Jennifer was one of the best reporters to work with. She's not... she wasn't a diva."

Danny smiled. "No, she wasn't. What can you tell me about what happened to her today?"

"Some piece of shit set her on fire and watched her burn. What do you think happened?"

"What can you tell me about the piece of shit?"

"Some batshit motherfucker who made me think I was batshit myself."

"How so?"

"Because I couldn't see him. Neither could Jennifer. We heard him but we couldn't see anything. We just saw..."

"What'd you see?"

"Some kind of shadow. I don't know, man." Spencer rubbed his eyes. "I still don't get it. Jennifer and I both heard him saying some creepy shit but we couldn't see him. Then next thing I knew she burst into flames."

Spencer's shaking increased and he wrapped the blanket the paramedic had given him tighter across his shoulders.

"What was he saying?" Danny asked.

"I don't know. Some foreign language I guess. I couldn't understand a word of it."

"Did it sound like anything familiar?"

Spencer shook his head. "Nothing I've ever heard. But all the while Jennifer was burning, he kept yelling . Then I heard him say some word like 'stee' and all of the sudden the fire just stopped. I never saw the son of a bitch."

"Did you hear anyone else? Maybe he had someone with him helping him stay hidden?"

"Naw, it wasn't like that. It was just him. It was like magic or something. I don't know how he did it." Spencer let out a deep breath and glanced up and down the street, where a crowd had now gathered. "This street was completely deserted when we got here. Nobody here but Jennifer and me. I tried to help her, I swear I did. But the flames were so goddamn hot I couldn't get near her. I didn't know what to do."

"I don't think there was anything you could have done, Mr. Spencer. Did you get hurt?"

"I've got a few burns. Nothing bad."

"Detective?"

Danny looked up to see the paramedic who had been monitoring Spencer standing over him.

"Yes?"

"Can I speak to you, please?"

Danny stood up and followed the paramedic a few feet away from Spencer.

"We need to take Mr. Spencer to the hospital. We're concerned about his mental state. He's been through a terrible shock."

"You're concerned because he's saying he couldn't see the guy, right?"

"He said the assailant was invisible. We need to have him evaluated by a physician."

"I understand. But you might want to evaluate me too because I think he's right. I think the guy was invisible when he did this."

"Detective?"

Danny shook his head. "Never mind. I've got enough from Mr. Spencer for now. Go ahead and take him in."

He returned to Jack and Tessa, who were talking with two uniformed officers.

"Don't tell me, let me guess," Jack said. "He didn't see anyone even though he was right here with Jennifer when she burned to death."

"You're right. He says he saw a shadow and he heard the guy chanting."

"Chanting what?"

Danny shrugged. "He doesn't know. But he says it was another language, just like the kids at the baseball game said. He says he heard a word that sounded like "stee" just as the fire stopped."

"Stee?"

"Something like that."

Anthony Rizzo joined the group, leaving the medical examiner and her team to investigate the corpse. The forensic investigators had also arrived on the scene and were combing the sidewalk for evidence.

"Oh Christ I know what you're going to say too," Jack said to Rizzo.

"Yeah, you probably do," Rizzo replied. "No signs of an accelerant. Nothing combustible."

"How is this son of a bitch doing this?" Jack asked. "It's like he's some kind of magician."

"That might be worth looking into, sir," Tessa said. "Maybe he's trained in magic tricks. He knows how to create illusions."

"Aww Jesus."

Danny remained silent, remembering the paramedic's reaction to Spencer's testimony. He couldn't say what he now knew to be true. This guy used magic, yes, but it was nothing close to the David Copperfield variety.

Jack raised his head and glanced around the street, pointing towards a nearby surveillance camera. "Maybe we can get something from that. Surely this guy isn't the goddamn invisible man walking down the street. And I don't see how he could stand wearing a hoodie again and covering up in this heat today." He wiped beads of sweat from his brow and gestured towards the ever-growing crowd of observers. "Otherwise let's just start canvassing. Somebody had to see something here."

\*\*\*\*

# Chapter 32

Danny sat at his desk and cursed himself repeatedly for ignoring Aleksei's suggestion of black magic as the cause of the fires. He had let Nechayev get under his skin enough to make him question his own instincts, a failure which may have resulted in Jennifer Higgin's absolutely horrific death. Instead of pursuing the idea that the murderer was using some sort of magic to burn people alive, Danny had spent weeks combing through old arson cases and digging up absolutely nothing. He may as well have been sitting around with his thumb up his ass.

That failure wouldn't happen again.

Tessa was with Anthony Rizzo in the conference room going through the files on Max Fugate, Nick Torrance, and Richard Phillips in desperation. Danny could see Jack on the phone in his office trying to convince the chief that he and his detectives had been doing everything humanly possible to solve the Fairbanks fire murders. The majority of the uniformed officers had long since gone home, replaced by the skeleton crew who worked the night shift. Danny was as alone as he was ever likely to get at the office.

He opened his desk drawer and pulled out the torn piece of paper he had scribbled the phone number on last month. He briefly wondered what time it was in Australia, but then realized he didn't give a rat's ass about interrupting Aleksei's sleep or lack thereof. As he fingered the paper, he was suddenly back at the Snow Creek resort, tied to the post of a bed and slowly freezing to death. He heard Aleksei's laughter as he shut the door on Danny and left him to his fate. He saw Aleksei smile, revealing the fangs that had dripped with the blood of countless young women.

"Goddammit, grow a pair, Fitzpatrick," he said, thankful that no one was around to hear him talking to himself. Taking a deep breath,

Danny swallowed his fear and punched the numbers into his phone. The phone rang and rang until he was about to hang up. He pulled the phone away from his ear when he heard the voice.

"Hello, Detective Fitzpatrick."

Danny returned the phone to his ear. "How'd you know it was me?"

"Because you're the only person I gave the number to. Actually, you're the main reason I got the phone. I don't have much of an interest in talking on it."

Danny was silent as the fear of the frigid and dark December pulsed through him.

"What can I do for you?" Aleksei asked. "How's the case?"

"What do you know about black magic?" Danny asked. "Or at least fire-starting magic?"

"Has there been another victim? I'm afraid I got a little bored and wasn't following along as closely. What have you and your colleagues been doing up there? It's no surprise that most of them are simpletons but I know you're much sharper. Have your skills dulled? Or was it just me you were so diligent about?"

"Answer my question."

"What was it again?"

"Tell me what you know about fire magic, asshole."

"It's humorous that you're so rude when you're calling me for help."

"Goddammit, Nechayev."

"Oh, alright, alright. What can I tell you? I know that there are extremely powerful witches who have the ability to cast spells that create fire."

"What about the ability to make themselves invisible?"

"I can't say I know anything about that, but with this kind of magic I wouldn't rule it out."

"What do you mean 'this kind of magic?' What do you know about it?"

"I know it's very powerful. Which I believe I already said. And I've seen a witch like this in action."

Danny scowled. Christ, this was like pulling teeth. He glanced in Jack's office and was relieved to see him still on the phone.

"Will you just tell me what you know, you son of a bitch?"

"When I first came to Alaska I met a man named Vasyl Dzubenko who ran a saloon called The Turnagain Arm. Do you know that area, the Turnagain Arm?"

"I've heard of it. Tell me about the saloon keeper."

"Fine. I worked for Mr. Dzubenko and learned English while in his employ. Unbeknownst to me he was a witch whose family had power that went back centuries. He knew about me and my kind and he tried to use his magic to kill me."

"By setting you on fire?"

"Yes."

"If only he had been successful," Danny said. "Think how many lives would have been saved."

"He came very close to being successful. But fortunately for me I had an idiot in my corner who killed him before he could burn me to a crisp."

"Wait a minute," Danny said, a thought tickling his memory. "What did you say his name was?"

"Vasyl Dzubenko."

"Was he Russian too?"

"Yes. Although, he called himself Ukrainian. Why?"

Danny rubbed his forehead. What was it about that name? "No reason. So how did he do it? How did he start the fire?"

"With a spell. He called upon some god of black magic and started chanting. Next thing I knew my feet and legs were on fire."

"He was chanting? What was he chanting?"

"I don't remember. I was slightly panicked at the time since I had flames dancing up my legs."

"How do you say stop in Russian?" Danny asked, changing gears.

"Stop."

"Yeah? So it's the same word?"

"Close enough. Why?"

"What about Ukrainian? Anything that sounds like stee?"

"I'm not overly familiar with that pedestrian language. But possibly Stiy."

"Does that mean stop?"

"Yes."

"What else can you tell me about this Dzubenko?"

"Not much. He had a grimoire he used for his magic."

"A grim what?"

"A grimoire."

"What the hell is that?"

"A book of spells. From the little I saw of it, I'd say Dzubenko's book went way back. This kind of magic is very old."

"Can people learn this magic?"

"You mean people who aren't witches? No. You have to be born with that kind of power."

"When did all this happen? When did you work for Dzubenko?"

"After I left St. Petersburg. During the building of the Alaskan railroad."

"How the hell do I know when you left St. Petersburg? And I sure as hell don't know when the Alaskan rail was built. You want to give me a year?"

"It was 1917."

"And you say Dzubenko was killed? Did he have any children?"

"No, but he had a wife. I let her live because killing her would have been an inconvenience for me. Why do you ask about children?"

"I guess I'm just wondering if this witch could have passed on his talent."

"His wife could have been pregnant at the time her husband died, I don't know. I never saw her again so I can't help you there." Aleksei paused. "Do you think you have a witch on the loose in Fairbanks?"

"I have no idea. I know I've got some kind of monster on the loose. A witch makes as much sense as anything else."

"You know the whole idea of witches wearing black hats and riding on brooms is nonsense, right? If you're hunting for a witch, that's not what you're looking for."

"Yeah, I think I can figure that out. Jesus Christ."

"Just trying to help."

"Believe it or not, Nechayev, you have been very helpful." Danny saw Jack hanging up the phone and getting up from his chair. He'd be on his way out here, no doubt.

"You'll let me know what you find, won't you?"

"You can read about it online, I'm sure," Danny said.

He disconnected the call without saying goodbye and put his phone back in his pocket and the slip of paper back in his drawer. He didn't want to have to explain his latest lead. And he needed time to process it, anyway. There was something about the name Dzubenko, he knew it. He just had to figure out what that something was.

****

# Chapter 33

Danny sat on his couch with Sox on his lap, a beer in one hand and a cigarette in the other. He took a drag from the cigarette and let the smoke sit in his mouth before blowing it out in a perfectly formed "O." He'd just hung up from a phone call with Amanda, who'd informed him she had definitely decided to stay in Sitka for the rest of the summer due to her mother's continued health problems. Danny thought that was a good idea considering the ongoing fires. There was no doubt that Fairbanks was a dangerous place to be at the moment.

Amanda had asked Danny about the case but he hadn't felt like talking about it. He didn't feel like doing anything at all. In fact, he had even turned off his television and was now merely staring at the wall opposite him. He longed to sleep, but each time he closed his eyes he saw the grotesque shell that was all that remained of Jennifer Higgins.

He took a long drink of beer and set the now empty bottle on the end table next to him. Finishing his cigarette, he stamped out the bud in the ash tray and reached for the open pack on the table. He stopped himself, once again remembering Jennifer's corpse. As sleepy as he was, he didn't need to set a fire and burn himself to death as well. Or worse, burn Sox. Danny hadn't cared what happened to him for quite a while now. But he did care about his dog.

Letting his head rest against the back of the couch, Danny closed his eyes and massaged Sox's ears in an effort to calm his mind. He felt himself drifting into dreams and was once again lost in the snow.

The snow was waist deep and he had forgotten to wear snowshoes. He sunk into the white landscape with each step, eventually winding up stuck in a drift that towered over him. The snow surrounded him, pulling him into the drift and turning his body to ice. He heard a man laughing and turned to see Aleksei standing next to the drift, his fangs bared and his head thrown back in laughter.

The snow was like water pulling Danny down and he knew he was going to drown in it. Aleksei continue to chuckle and didn't try to hide his glee as Danny sank deeper and deeper into the whiteness.

"Dzubenko," Aleksei said between guffaws. "Remember? Vasyl Dzubenko."

Danny jumped straight up and knocked Sox from his lap. The frightened dog whimpered and looked up at him with his tail between his legs.

"I'm sorry buddy," Danny said.

He reached a trembling hand out to the dog. Never one to hold a grudge, Sox responded by licking Danny's hand with his warm and wet tongue. He thumped his tail as Danny returned to massaging his ears.

"Why do I know the name Dzubenko, Sox?"

His fingers froze mid-massage as he suddenly remembered the answer to his question. There was a Dzubenko in the old arson cases he had been going through. A fire back in the 1990s....

Danny leaped up from the couch and grabbed his keys from their place on the rack next to his door.

"I have to go back into work," he said to his now clearly perturbed and confused dog. "You go ahead and go back to sleep."

Danny ignored Sox's irritated bark as he left his apartment and headed for his car. It was 2:00 in the morning and the sun had set a few hours ago, giving Danny and the rest of Fairbanks a short break from the unrelenting heat. Twilight bathed the night sky in waves of pink and lavender. He got in the car and quickly drove off towards the police station with the rush of adrenalin that always came with the knowledge that he had found the break that had previously eluded him.

He was glad he'd had this revelation in the middle of the night when he could work largely undisturbed. The night shift wouldn't ask any questions and he would easily have the records room to himself. He couldn't help but wish he could simply bring up the file he wanted on the computer, but the reports from the 1990s hadn't been digitized yet. It was a good bet that they never would be, considering the Fairbanks' department's limited budget and manpower. There were much more important things to focus on.

Danny now knew exactly the case he was looking for and he didn't think it would take him long to find it again. He pressed his foot to the floor and careened through the eerily empty Fairbanks streets.

\*\*\*\*

# Chapter 34

*August 1, 2013*

"Danny, what on earth are you doing? Have you been here all night?"

Danny turned in his chair to see Tessa standing behind him.

"Close enough," he said.

Tessa eyed his rumpled blue shirt and khaki pants, which were the same clothes he had worn yesterday, as well as his tangled hair and bloodshot eyes.

"Have you been drinking again?"

"What? No. Or at least I haven't been since around 2:00. I've been working."

Tessa sat down at her own desk. "How so?"

"I decided to go back to the old arson cases I'd been looking at before Jennifer was killed. I couldn't sleep so why the hell not, right?" Danny pointed to the open folder on his desk. "And I found an interesting one."

"What is it?"

"In 1996 a house over on McHenry Street that belonged to a family named Dzubenko burned to the ground. The parents and two of their three children were all killed. One boy, a 12-year-old named Jamie, survived. The investigators could never figure out what started the fire. The scene they describe sounds just like the broken record Anthony keeps giving us after each of our fires now."

Tessa made no effort to hide her interest. "What happened to the boy?"

"He went to live with a relative but I don't know what happened from there. But I do know that a Jamie Dzubenko who would be the age he is now works in the lab at Fairbanks General."

"Where Max Fugate worked..."

"Exactly."

"But what made you zero in on this case? There's something else. Something you're not telling me."

"Damn right," Danny thought. "And I'm not going to either."

"Danny?" Tessa asked. "What aren't you telling me?"

"One of the investigators viewed Jamie as a suspect and believed that he started the fire that killed his family, but he couldn't ever prove it. I want to talk to him and see why he thought that."

Danny hoped that answer would be enough to satisfy Tessa.

"Who's the investigator?"

"His name is Frank Wainscott. He retired fifteen years ago but he still lives in Fairbanks."

"Let's go talk to him then."

"I'd rather do this on my own. I thought you were doing the press conference with the chief this morning anyway."

"You're supposed to be doing that too. And why would you want to do this alone?"

Danny ignored the question and got up from his chair. "Well we can't both miss the press conference, can we? I'll just take care of this visit this morning and catch you up on it later."

"Danny, what's this about?"

"It's about finally meeting someone who could give us some insight into this case." He turned his back on his partner and walked towards the exit. "I need to take a quick shower so I don't scare Wainscott when I show up at his house. I'll meet you back here this afternoon."

****

# Chapter 35

Danny drove up to Frank Wainscott's colonial style home on 21st street and pulled into the driveway. Wainscott apparently liked bright colors, as the house was painted a vivid blue shade that must have made the home stand out like a sore thumb when it was surrounded by snow in the winter. Maybe that was the point. Wainscott wanted to bring a bit of cheer to the long and dark winters. In contrast to the blue, the garage and door were painted white. A German shepherd dog sat in Wainscott's large fenced-in yard, cocking his ears and running to the fence when he saw Danny walking up the sidewalk to the porch. His loud bark alerted his owner to Danny's presence before Danny even had a chance to ring the doorbell.

A stooped and grey haired man opened the white door and gazed at him warily. "Are you Detective Fitzpatrick?"

"I am, sir. Thanks for agreeing to talk with me."

Wainscott opened the door wider to allow Danny inside. "I'm happy to do it. But it's hard for me to believe I know anything that can help you. I've been retired a long time."

"That's a handsome dog you've got out there," Danny said. "I'm a dog lover myself."

"That's Riley. He was my wife's dog really, but now that she's gone I'm glad to have his company."

Danny followed Wainscott into a spacious living room decorated in neutral tones of beige and white.

"How long has your wife been gone?" he asked.

"Six months. Please, make yourself comfortable and have a seat."

Danny sat down on a champagne colored sofa. "I'm sorry for your loss. I can imagine you must miss her terribly."

"You married?"

"I was. My wife was murdered a few years ago."

Wainscott let out a breath and sat down across from Danny in a hard-back wing chair. "Well I'm sorry to you too then. That's rough."

"It was. Is," Danny paused, "But I didn't come here to talk about my personal problems or yours, sir."

"Right. So what is it you did come here to talk about, Detective?"

"Danny, please."

"Then call me Frank."

"Okay, Frank. I want to talk to you about an unsolved arson case from the 1990s. The Dzubenko family."

A shadow crossed Frank's face. "That was a tough one."

"Will you tell me about it?"

"Both parents and two youngsters were killed. The oldest boy, Jamie, he made it out. When we got to the scene he was standing there watching the house burn. Kid had the weirdest damn look on his face I've ever seen."

"How so?"

"He almost looked happy. Or at least content. At first I thought the kid was just in shock. But he stayed that way. When they carried the bodies of his family out he didn't react at all. No crying, no sign of horror. I swore I saw him smile when they brought out the last body – that of his little sister."

Frank paused and shook his head at the memory. "Can I get you a cup of coffee?" he asked, abruptly changing the subject.

"No, thank you. I've had more than my share this morning. But I'll wait here if you'd like to get a cup for yourself."

"No, no, I'm fine." Frank stared at the wall above Danny's head and let his mind retreat into the past.

"That kid stood there on his lawn holding a book. According to the neighbors who called 911 he walked out of the burning house clutching that book to his chest and looking like he had all the time in the world. They came running out of their house asking if he was okay and he just stared at them, and then stared down at his book. He wouldn't speak to them or to us when we arrived."

"What was the book he had?"

"I don't know. Some kind of crazy crap about magic supposedly. It was in a foreign language so I couldn't even read it. But two of the neighbor kids told us Jamie had been reading it obsessively for months and had told them it was his great-grandfather's magic book. The kids all thought he was nuts. I've thought ever since that they were right."

"What happened to Jamie?"

"He went to live with an aunt in Anchorage. I never had any further contact with the boy after that. But I thought back then that he started the fire himself. I would have bet my life savings on it. But I didn't have a shred of evidence to back my feelings up."

"From what I read in your report, the arson team never figured out what started the fire."

"That's right, they didn't. Not a goddamn clue. And to make it worse, there seemed to be multiple starting points for the fire in various parts of the house. They couldn't even determine the point of origin. It was the strangest damn thing any of us had ever seen. You would have thought the fire started by magic."

"What did Jamie say when you asked him about the fire?"

"He said he was sound asleep and woke up to one of the smoke alarms going off. His room was on the first floor of the house while the rest of the family slept upstairs. Jamie said he heard his mother screaming for his sister and tried to run upstairs but couldn't make it through the smoke. He claimed he got so frightened he just ran outside."

"What about the book?"

"That was one of the reasons I questioned his story. He forgot about the book when he was first telling us what happened. When I asked him about it, he said he grabbed it before he left his room and tried to go upstairs. Now you tell me, what youngster wakes up to the sound of a smoke alarm and the smell of fire and grabs a goddamn book when he's supposedly going to run upstairs to help his family? It didn't make a damn bit of sense." Frank scowled in anger as if the fire had just happened yesterday. "He just insisted he really loved his book and its connection to his family history and he didn't want to lose it."

"I can see why you questioned it."

"Anyone would have. But there wasn't anything else to go on, you know? And how do you go about accusing a kid who just lost his whole family in a fire? The media painted it as a tragedy of course, which it was, but he became their star victim. People were lining up to donate money to help the kid. And who could blame them? On the surface, he had been through an unimaginable hell and had seen his whole family die. But there was more to it, I was sure of it."

"What made you so certain though? Weird or surprising things like grabbing the book do happen when people are frightened."

"Right, they do. But it was just the demeanor of this kid. I always got the sense he was enjoying the attention and loving the fact that he was putting one over on everybody. He never showed any sign of grief or pain or sorrow. He never showed any emotion at all. There was something wrong with that kid, I knew it. Hell, I still know it."

"What you know and what you can prove are two very different things sometimes, aren't they?"

"They sure as hell are." Frank shifted in his chair. "Now it's my turn to ask you some questions. You're asking about this case because of the fires this summer, aren't you?"

"Sure am. We're desperate for anything on this. We don't have a clue who is killing these people or how they're starting the fires to do it."

"It's horrible, that's for sure. Just hearing it on the news makes me glad I'm retired."

Danny smiled. "I kind of wish I was."

"Well, I wish I could help you, Danny, I really do. I know what it's like to be stuck in the middle of a nightmare and have no idea how to stop it."

"You've been a big help, Frank. I'm not sure how yet, but I can feel it."

Frank chuckled and stood up from his chair. "I know about that too. Sometimes a feeling is all you need."

Danny followed his lead and got up from the couch. "Thank you again for meeting with me."

"I was glad to do it. Sometimes it feels good to talk to another cop again. You come back any time."

"I may just take you up on that offer."

Danny pulled his phone from his pocket and turned it off as he walked out of Frank's home and returned to his car. He knew Tessa would be calling him and would also be mad as hell when he didn't answer, but he couldn't worry about that now. He needed to go home before going back to the station, as he had some research he wanted to do on his own computer without anyone interrupting him or looking over his shoulder.

He needed to find out more about Jamie Dzubenko's life after his family had been killed in the mysterious house fire. And he wanted to know more about Aleksei's long-ago nemesis with the same last name. He knew there was a connection. There had to be.

****

# Chapter 36

"Danny, where in the hell have you been?"

Danny didn't even make it to his desk before Tessa's angry voice assaulted his eardrums.

"I told you I was going to see that retired cop."

"Right. How many hours ago was that? And why the hell weren't you answering your phone?"

Danny pulled his phone from his pocket and sheepishly turned it on.

"Sorry, I don't know how this got turned off."

Tessa rolled her eyes. "You are so full of shit."

"Alright, alright, I turned it off, I admit it. I was just following a lead and I wanted a little time to explore it on my own without my phone interrupting me every five minutes."

"So you just cut your partner out of the case?"

"You know, as I recall, the last partner I had murdered my wife. Maybe I work better alone."

"And as I recall, the last time you worked alone you almost died and I had to fly to the Arctic in the dead of winter to save your sorry ass."

Danny couldn't help but laugh. He held up his hands in surrender.

"Fine. You win. But I'm not cutting you out of anything. I was hoping I could share what I found with you now."

Tessa sat down at her desk as Danny took his own seat.

"Alright," she said. "What do you have?"

"Jamie Dzubenko is the guy whose family got killed in the fire, I told you that, right?"

"You did."

"So I talked with Frank Wainscott this morning. The fire happened not too many years before he retired. He was always convinced that

Jamie did it, but he could never prove it. He didn't have a shred of evidence. But he still believes it with all his heart."

"Why?"

"Because the kid was standing outside just watching the house burn when they arrived on the scene. He was clutching a book he took from his room before he ran outside. Frank said he just acted strange, even for someone who would obviously be traumatized and in shock. He said the kid never once showed any sense of sadness or grief or horror over what happened. If anything, he merely seemed to relish all the attention he got after the tragedy."

"How did the fire start?"

"That's the other interesting piece. They never figured out how it started. The arson report was the same kind of bullcrap Anthony keeps telling us now. As far as anyone could tell, nothing caused the fire. But it burned down a house and killed four people inside it."

Danny took a deep breath and gathered his thoughts before continuing his story. He knew he had to present the next bit of information very carefully for Tessa to take him seriously.

"You remember when you mentioned magicians and how they use illusion in their acts? You were wondering if our guy might be into something like that to hide himself."

"Yeah. I think that shows how absolutely desperate I am to find something that makes sense in these murders."

"Well I'm right there with you. And here's the thing. Frank said the book Jamie brought out of his house and clung to like it was his lifeline was some kind of magic book. The kid said it belonged to his great-grandparents. But it wasn't written in English so Frank never actually read it. He thought it was in Russian from what he remembered." Danny paused again. "Remember the chanting the kids at the park heard? They said it didn't sound like any of the Romance languages. And Bob heard something that sounded like 'stee.' That could be Russian or a similar language."

"Could be."

"I did a little digging and looked into Jamie's family tree. His great-grandfather was a man named Vasyl Dzubenko who came to Alaska from Russia in the early 20th century. He ran a saloon that traveled with the Alaskan railroad while it was being built. He was actually Ukrainian, something he was very proud of. He died in 1917 but his wife Lara survived and moved to Fairbanks. She was pregnant when her husband died and had a son after she moved here. The family stayed in the city and eventually Lara's grandson had Jamie in 1984."

"What does this prove?"

"I looked up how you say 'stop' in Ukrainian. It sounds an awful lot like the 'stee' Bob heard as the fire stopped. I think the magic book Jamie kept belonged to his great-grandfather Vasyl. He's Ukrainian, not Russian, and it's Ukrainian that he's chanting when he kills these people."

"But how is he starting the fires?"

"I don't know that yet. But I think you were on to something about the magic." Danny pulled some books from a bag he had carried to his desk. "I actually stopped on my way here and got some books about magic at the library. I want to see if I can find something that helps us figure out how he's creating this illusion. What do you think?"

"It's interesting, that's for sure. So Frank was dead certain about Jamie?"

"Absolutely. Said he's is still haunted by the kid standing there watching his home and family burn like he didn't have a care in the world."

"Maybe you and I should go have a talk with Jamie Dzubenko. See if we can get a feel for him ourselves. We could say we're meeting with people who knew Max Fugate. And that we're looking into previous suspicious fires in the city."

"That'll work. He won't buy it but that's okay. We're just going to be talking to him."

"Want to head over to the hospital and see if he's working?"

"Sounds good to me."

Danny stood up and rubbed his hands together, excited to have a lead to follow. The thundering voice of his boss interrupted his plans.

"Glad to see you here, Fitzpatrick," Jack said. "Nice of you to make it in. Tessa called you how many times?"

"Sorry about that, Captain. I was following up on a lead and didn't realize my phone was turned off."

Jack rolled his eyes in exactly the same manner Tessa had. "Bullshit. I don't know what you were up to and I really don't give a shit if it gives us something to latch on to in this case. Because believe it or not, it just got worse."

"Oh no," Tessa said. "Someone else has been killed?"

"No, not yet. But we did get another letter from our murderous arsonist." Jack waved a piece of white paper encased in an evidence bag. "He got in touch with us again."

Jack placed the clear evidence bag on Tessa's desk so the two detectives could see the letter and its message.

"Do you think Jennifer Higgins and the Reverend Phillips guessed correctly?" was written across the top of the page in the same precise print that had been on the previous letter.

"This son of a bitch," Danny said. "He did write 'who do you think is next?' last time, didn't he?"

"He did. Obviously he thinks he's being funny now," Jack said.

"There's more though," Tessa said, pointing to an amateurish pencil drawing of a fire in the middle of the page. An unskilled hand had drawn orange and red flames across the paper. Below the drawing was another question. "Are you ready for Vulcanalia?"

"What the hell is Vulcanalia?" Danny asked.

"No idea," Jack answered.

"I guess we better find out," Tessa said.

She sat back down at her desk and booted up her computer. Her eyes scanned the results of her google search.

"Oh my God," she said, her voice barely above a whisper.

"What is it?" Jack asked, trying to read the screen over Tessa's shoulder.

"Vulcanalia was a festival held every August in ancient Rome to honor Vulcan, the god of fire. The Romans set bonfires all over the city to honor him and threw animals into the fires as sacrifices."

"When in August?" Danny asked.

"August 23."

"So you think this is a warning that this horse's ass is going to set the city on fire on the 23?" Jack asked.

"I'd say that's a safe bet," Danny said. "And instead of animals, maybe he plans on using humans for the sacrifices. Maybe that's what he's already been doing."

"Aww, Jesus," Jack said. "See what I mean? It just keeps getting worse. So he's not only an arsonist who can apparently start fires out of thin air, he's also a batshit lunatic who's worshipping some ancient god. Christ Almighty."

"When was Max Fugate murdered?" Tessa asked.

"Late May. Why?" Danny responded.

"It says here that May 23 is also sacred to Vulcan."

"So I guess that's why he chose it as his starting date. If there was a way to determine exactly when Fugate died I'm sure we'd find out it was the 23. It had to be." Danny paused and rubbed his chin with his fingers. "Do you think he'll send this one to the media too, like he sent the last one to Jennifer?"

"I wouldn't be surprised," Jack said. "Why?"

"Because people are already in a state around here since Jennifer's murder, not to mention the Pioneer Park and Golden Days fires. The whole city is one millisecond away from being in a full-fledged panic. People can't figure out what's going on and if this gets out things are only going to get worse. It will be like a city under siege."

"But that's almost what it is, isn't it? If this lunatic plans to set fires all over the place, we will be under siege." Tessa shook her head. "Would it be better if it did get out so people have some warning? Maybe we should even try to evacuate the city."

Jack held up his hands. "Hold the phone. We don't have to do anything that drastic yet. We've still got time to catch this bastard." He turned towards Danny. "Did you say you found a new lead you were working on this morning?"

"Yeah. A guy named Jamie Dzubenko whose family was killed in a suspicious fire back in the 1990s. I talked to the investigator at the time and he thought Jamie set the fire but couldn't prove it."

"Who was the investigator?"

"Frank Wainscott."

"I knew him. Great cop."

"I trusted his instincts when I talked to him this morning. I think it's worth looking into this guy and seeing what he's been up to since."

"Good. Then you two get to it. This son of a bitch can't stay anonymous forever. I'm taking this letter down to the forensics team."

"We'll be in touch as soon as we talk to Dzubenko," Danny said.

Danny followed Tessa outside to his car. Steam rose from the heat of the blacktop as it baked in the mid-afternoon sun.

\*\*\*\*

# Chapter 37

Jamie sat on his couch with his laptop and browsed the local news sites for the latest on his activities. It appeared that the police had not shared his latest letter with the media and, as he had decided not to send them more communication himself, he felt sure that his plans for Vulcanalia were still known only to him. And to whichever police officers had read his letter and looked up the meaning of the word.

He glanced out his window at the large backyard he shared with his fellow tenant, the man who lived on the top floor of the house while Jamie lived on the bottom. Jamie had been so glad to find the house which was now two apartments. He wouldn't have been able to stand living in a large complex with all the noise that comes with families and children and pets. He loved the quiet ranch style house with grey siding and a two car garage that he and his upstairs neighbor shared.

Jamie couldn't remember ever feeling better than he did this summer. He continued to build up his strength with vitamins and exercise and he knew he was going to be prepared for Vulcanalia. He'd pull it off; there was no question about that. And his success throughout the summer was giving him more emotional strength than he'd ever known was possible. He supposed that was understandable considering he was fulfilling his destiny. The destiny that his parents had tried to deny him.

His contentment turned to irritation and surprise as he heard tires on the gravel driveway next to the house. No one ever visited here. Perhaps his neighbor was expecting company. But as far as Jamie knew, the neighbor was not even home as he always worked a regular nine to five job. Jamie walked to the other side of his living room and looked out the window that faced the drive. His nostrils flared with a rush of anger that quickly replaced his irritation. It was obvious to anyone with even half a brain that the tall white man and the small black woman who were getting out of their car and coming to his door were cops.

For a second, his anger turned to fear and he wondered if these were the cops who had read his letter. But they couldn't have figured out his identity from that. He'd made sure of that. There was no point in conjuring up nightmare scenarios. Especially when he had complete confidence in his abilities and he knew he hadn't screwed up. He couldn't imagine why these cops had turned up at his door but it had to be a coincidence.

The doorbell rang and Jamie quickly closed his laptop and set it on his desk before walking to answer the door.

"Yes?"

"Mr. Dzubenko?" the woman asked.

"Yes, that's me."

"I'm Detective Tessa Washington and this is my partner Detective Danny Fitzpatrick." Both the man and the woman flashed their badges. "Fairbanks PD. Can we talk to you?"

"What about?"

This time the man answered. "We're investigating the fire murders that have gone on this summer. We're hoping you may have some information that could help us."

Jamie clutched the doorknob to keep his hand steady. "I can't imagine what information I could have."

The male detective wedged his foot against Jamie's door, effectively blocking any effort Jamie might make to close it.

"We tried to find you at work but were told you're working the night shift tonight," he said. "I'm sure you've got things you need to do before you go to work. We won't take up too much of your time."

Jamie stepped back from the door and allowed the two cops inside. "Of course. Please come in." He closed the door and walked into his living room. "Please have a seat and make yourselves comfortable."

He sat down in the wing chair across from his couch, where the two detectives were now seated. "What can I help you with?"

"We're aware that your family was killed in a fire when you were young," the woman said. "And we're terribly sorry to have to bring up such a tragedy. I can't imagine what you must have gone through."

Jamie cleared his throat and tried his best to look pained. "Well, yes, it was terrible, of course. A day doesn't go by that I don't think of them all."

Jamie knew that was the sort of thing people said when they were grieving. At least he hoped it was.

"We're sorry for your loss," the male detective said. "The house burned down too, isn't that correct?"

"Yes, yes it is." Jamie paused and cleared his throat again. "May I ask what this has to do with your investigation? You must know how hard it is for me to talk about what happened to my family."

The man answered again. Jamie wished he could remember both of their names. What was his name again? Fitzpatrick?

"I'm sure it is and, again, we're terribly sorry. But the records from that fire indicate that no cause was ever found and the origins were listed as suspicious. We're looking into old fires that share traits with the cases we're investigating now."

"What traits could my family's case possibly share with what's happening now? My family died in 1996."

"Of course," the woman said. "But it's as Detective Fitzpatrick said. The origins of the fire that killed your family were listed as suspicious and the cause was unknown."

Jamie let out a breath. "Okay. But I really don't see how I can help you…"

"We know you were only 12 years old when this happened," Fitzpatrick said. "And you weren't able to provide the police with any information at that time. But I'm wondering if now, looking back on it, it's possible you can remember anything that could have been unusual in the time leading up to the fire. Anyone new involved with your family? Did your parents make any big purchases that were delivered to your home? Any work done in the house so that your parents had workmen in and out?"

Jamie pretended to search his memory before solemnly shaking his head. "No," he said. "I don't remember anything like that."

"Did your parents seem edgy or upset at all? Maybe stressed over something you couldn't have understood at that time."

"No," Jamie said sharply. "Honestly, detectives, I can't see what good can come out of making me relive this. I don't have anything to tell you now that I didn't already tell the detectives back then."

Fitzpatrick held up a hand. "I'm sorry, really, I am. This is a long shot but you have to understand, we're kind of desperate here. People are dying and we don't know why."

"I'd be happy to help you if I could."

The woman spoke up. "Did you know Max Fugate, Mr. Dzubenko?"

"Max Fugate? Is that the doctor who was killed?"

"Yes. Did you know him?"

"No. Why?"

"You both worked at the hospital. We thought you may have known each other, that's all."

Jamie shrugged. "It's a big hospital. I remember seeing him in the hallways and saying hello, but nothing beyond that. I only knew who he was because he was such a good surgeon. I'm sure he had no idea who I was."

The woman nodded. "Well, we knew it was a longshot."

To Jamie's relief, both detectives stood up from the couch. The woman fished in her purse and handed him a business card.

"Mr. Dzubenko, thank you so much for talking with us. We are sorry to have brought up such difficult memories for you. If you happen to think of anything that could help us, you've got my number there."

"Of course. I really do wish I could help. It's so terrible what's been happening."

"Yes it is. We'll see ourselves out."

Jamie watched the two detectives' backs through his window as they returned to their car. Anger rose in his throat as they got inside the car and chattered to each other. He wondered what game they were playing. Surely their reason for contacting him couldn't possibly be valid. And what cops would ever admit they were desperate to find something to go on in their investigation?

But there was no way they could be on to him. No one would believe in his magic, let alone be able to figure it out. Still, these cops had pissed him off and he didn't need the aggravation. He didn't need anything that took away from his emotional strength and stamina when it was so important to his efforts.

Maybe he had been wrong to only send his Vulcanlia plans to the police. He should let the whole city know what was coming and how powerless the police were to stop it. Jamie felt his anger dissipate and his previous calmness return to him. Why had he let the police upset him? It would be easy enough to get them off his back and make them so preoccupied they'd never have time to worry about decades-old fires. Jamie smiled as he imagined the consequences of what he was about to do. He'd send the police department into a tailspin.

****

# Chapter 38

"So what did you think of him?" Danny asked as he juggled steering his car and lighting a cigarette. He opened his window and let the smoke escape out of the car.

Tessa opened her own window, grimacing at the hot air that greeted her. "Damn when are we going to get a break from this heat?"

"I'm thinking September is the best we can hope for at this point. This feels more like a Chicago summer all the time."

"You know, I think I liked you better when drinking was your vice," Tessa said, waving her hand in front of her face in a futile attempt to banish the smoke. "This smoking has to stop. Or at least it has to stop when I'm in the car with you."

Danny took a final long drag on his cigarette and stamped it out in the ashtray underneath the car stereo. "Fine," he said. "I won't torture you. Now can we talk about Jamie Dzubenko?"

Tessa gratefully closed her window and reached over to turn up the air conditioning. She angled all of the vents she could reach in her direction.

"I think there's definitely something off with him" she said. "I can see why Frank Wainscott thought he started that fire himself."

Danny angled the air conditioning vents back towards his own seat. "Yeah. It felt like he was just saying what he thinks people say about a tragedy. His affect was flat and I didn't see a single emotion cross his face the whole time we were talking to him."

"He's a cold fish, no doubt about that."

"You did get a rise out of him by bringing up Max Fugate though."

"I thought so too. He was clearly surprised by that."

Danny turned left on Cushman Street and headed towards the police station. "Of course, we still don't have a damn thing on him."

"No. But at least we know we got under his skin a bit. Who knows, maybe if he is our guy and we rattled him he'll screw up."

"That would be nice. But we both know it's wishful thinking. Did you notice anything interesting about his apartment?"

Tessa shrugged. "It was obviously very tidy. And he had what looked like a stockpile of vitamins in his kitchen, did you see those?"

"Those bottles lined up in rows along the counter? Yeah. I guess he's a health nut."

"Or he's doing some sort of fitness regimen. Maybe training or building up his strength and going overboard on vitamins?"

"Could be," Danny said. "And if he's a runner himself that could be how he knew Max Fugate's pattern of jogging at Griffin Park. That might be something worth exploring more."

He turned into the station parking lot and pulled into a spot close to the door. He kept the car running, wanting to sit in the air conditioning as long as possible. Tessa made no move to get out of the car.

"Say he is our guy," she said. "How the hell is he doing this? How is he starting these fires?"

Danny flirted with the notion of telling her what he really believed but quickly shut that idea down. "I'm gonna go over those magic books and websites with a fine-toothed comb and see how magicians do it. You said it yourself, it's an illusion. Granted, this guy's got Houdini beat all to hell if he's pulling something like this off, but I don't know where else to look right now."

Tessa stared at the door of the station and willed herself to get out of the car and into the heat. Her will wasn't strong enough. "You know, I actually think it's getting hotter every damn day. It's like we're living in hell here."

"Unfortunately I don't think we're far from our city turning into a literal hell if we can't find our friendly neighborhood arsonist and stop him. Should we go inside and see what Jack has managed to find out about the latest letter?"

"Want to bet his answer will be not a damn thing?"

"I'd say that's a safe bet. But come on, we can't put it off any longer."

Danny turned off the ignition and the two detectives stepped out into the heat.

****

# Chapter 39

Danny would never have wished Tessa harm or sickness, in fact she was probably the last person on earth to whom he would want anything bad to happen. But he still couldn't deny he was relieved when she called him that morning and let him know that she would not be able to accompany him to Anchorage to interview Constance Davenport, the aunt Jamie Dzubenko had gone to live with after the fire that killed his family. Danny had looked into Jamie's history after Frank Wainscott had mentioned the aunt and learned that less than a year after moving to Anchorage Jamie had returned to Fairbanks, where he spent his teenage years in foster care.

Danny and Tessa had planned to travel to Anchorage this morning to meet Constance Davenport, but a migraine had felled Tessa and she simply couldn't leave her apartment until it subsided. Danny remembered the migraines his mother had suffered from and knew Tessa meant what she said. She wouldn't be in any shape to fly in an airplane, let alone to interview anyone.

But Danny was glad to be going alone, as now he could interview Constance without worrying about veering into magic if he sensed she was on the same page that he was about Jamie Dzubenko. From the phone conversation he had already had with her, Danny believed that she was. She was afraid of Jamie, that much was clear. Danny had a feeling Constance was afraid because she knew about the magic that ran through her family tree. And she knew it wasn't the kind of magic Tessa thought they were investigating.

He frowned as the low gas indicator sounded on his dashboard and cursed himself for forgetting to fill up the night before. Glancing at the dashboard clock, he was relieved to realize he had plenty of time to get gas now before his flight. The last thing he needed was to forget to fill up when he got back to Fairbanks later this evening and wind up

running out of gas on the street. He drove into the Airport Gas & Oil lot and pulled up to the closest pump.

"Detective Fitzpatrick?"

Danny turned towards the sound of a woman's voice as he pumped his gas. He was surprised to see Maria Treibel, the woman he had saved from Aleksei Nechayev several months earlier.

"Ms. Treibel. How are you?"

The tall and slender woman pushed a strand of blond hair from her pretty face. "I'm fine. And it's Maria, please."

"Maria," Danny said, smiling. "You look great."

"No doubt much better than the last time you saw me."

"No doubt. I'm so glad."

"How are you?" Maria asked. "From what I remember you were hurt too."

"I'm totally fine. It wasn't anything serious."

Maria stared at him with the blue eyes that had looked nearly lifeless when he had last seen her in her hospital bed.

"I'm glad I ran into you," she said. "I thought about calling you before I left but I didn't think it was appropriate…"

"Left? You're going somewhere?"

"Yeah. I'm on my way to the airport, actually."

"Well I am too. I guess that's a safe bet considering we're both at Airport Oil & Gas."

Maria smiled. "Where are you headed?"

"Just to Anchorage for work. How about you?"

"I'm going to San Francisco. I'm moving there."

"Really?"

"Yeah. I got a photography job with San Fran Weekly. And I'm still going to be doing my freelance work."

"Sounds great. I've never been to the famous City by the Bay."

"I have. I grew up in Sacramento and visited San Francisco many times. I loved it. Not that I have anything against Fairbanks really. But I just couldn't… I can't stay here anymore."

"Because of what happened to you?"

"Because of Aleksei, yes," Maria said, spitting out the words as if they had been lodged in her throat for far too long. She let out a deep breath and stared out into the passing traffic. "Nate and I aren't seeing each other anymore. We broke up not long after I got out of the hospital."

"I'm sorry to hear that."

Maria shrugged. "It was a long time coming anyway. But there's nothing to hold me here now. And I just can't..."

Danny put his hand on Maria's arm. "It's okay. You don't have to talk about it."

"I see him everywhere I look. Everywhere I go. I keep thinking he'll show up again."

"I don't believe he will. He's gone. He's far away from Alaska now, I'm sure of it."

"When I try to sleep, I dream about him. I dream that's he's captured me again..."

"I'm sorry," Danny said. "I've had nightmares of him too."

Maria looked up into Danny's face and an understanding passed between their eyes. "When we were at the hospital you asked me if I had seen anything strange about Aleksei. If I knew there was something different about him."

"Maria, you don't have to talk about this."

"I did," Maria said, ignoring Danny's protests. "I knew what you were asking about. I know what he is. You do too, don't you?"

Danny sighed. "I do," he said.

"I haven't told anyone. No one would believe me."

"I know. I don't talk about it either."

Maria broke his gaze and returned to staring at the passing cars. "Thank you for saving my life," she said.

"I was just doing my job. And several other cops who were doing their jobs saved both of us."

Maria turned back to him. "If it wasn't for you, I'd be one of the women they're finding up in the Arctic now. One of those dead bodies frozen up there."

Danny swallowed a lump in his throat. "I'm glad you're not," he said.

"I should go now. My flight..."

Danny removed the nozzle from his gas tank and returned it to the pump. "I need to get going too," he said. "I'm glad I got to see you, Maria. And I hope you make a great life for yourself in San Francisco.

142

You deserve it."

Maria blinked back tears. She stood on tiptoes and brushed Danny's cheek with her lips. "Thank you," she whispered.

Before Danny could respond, she had returned to her car. He watched her pull out of the lot without looking back in his direction.

\*\*\*\*

# Chapter 40

Danny walked up the sidewalk of Constance Davenport's home, a two story white wood frame house with a large satellite dish on its roof. He rang the doorbell and within seconds a woman opened the door.

"Detective Fitzpatrick?" she asked.

Danny presented her his badge. "In the flesh," he said. "Are you Constance Davenport?"

"I am."

Constance opened the door and invited Danny in to the artic entry, a small "in between" room that most houses in Alaska had to separate their front door from their living space. While the room wasn't necessary in the summer, it was crucial to keeping the rest of the house warm in the winter when the temperature outside was in the single digits or worse.

"If this were the winter I'd ask to take your coat," Constance said. "But I know you don't have one today."

"You're getting the same heat wave we are, clearly," Danny said. "It sucks, doesn't it?"

"It does. I'm actually eager for winter."

Constance opened the door of the entry and led Danny into the living room of her house. She was a short woman who had probably once been thin but now bore the weight of bearing several children. Her brown hair was pulled into a pony-tail at the nape of her neck.

"Can I offer you something to drink?" she asked.

"No, thank you. I'm fine."

"Have a seat then, please," Constance said, pointing towards a large and comfortable looking brown leather sofa. She took a seat herself in a matching recliner.

Danny sank into the sofa and was pleased to find it was as comfortable as it appeared. The cramped airplane seat had given his long legs fits in spite of the fact that his flight had barely taken an hour.

"Thanks for agreeing to meet with me," he said.

"I don't mind. Although I don't know what I can tell you about my nephew. I haven't seen him in years."

"I understand that. But I'm interested in what happened when he stayed here with you after the fire. He didn't stay too long, did he?"

Constance turned red. "No, he didn't. But I tried, I really did. You have to understand, I had my own children to think about."

"Mrs. Davenport, I'm not accusing you of anything, trust me. I'm merely trying to find out what happened. Why did you send Jamie back to Fairbanks?"

Constance stared down at the hands she twisted together in her lap. "I was afraid of him," she said, her voice barely audible. "God help me, he was my brother's child and I wanted to care for him but I simply couldn't."

"Why were you afraid of him?"

"He wasn't right. I can't explain it, but I knew from the day he came to us that there was something wrong with him. I tried to attribute it to grief but it wasn't that. It wasn't…" Constance paused and bit her lip. "I didn't even know the child when he came to live with us. My husband George got a job here in Anchorage when Jamie was only a year old. We always meant to return to Fairbanks but we have four children and when the kids were young things always seemed to get in the way of any plans we made. Plus, a six-hour drive isn't a picnic with kids and it was too expensive for us all to fly. Robert and I always kept in touch over the phone and through letters but I didn't know his kids and he didn't know mine. But of course when we lost him I wanted to take Jamie in. I was devastated at how my brother died. And I couldn't imagine how that poor boy was going to be able to cope with what had happened to his family. I had to try to help him. I thought he could at least have a family here with us."

"It didn't turn out that way, obviously."

"No, it didn't. Almost from the moment he arrived, he behaved strangely. I'd hear him in his room chanting in a foreign language. And he never wanted to do anything but read my grandfather's old book."

"Did you know what that book was?"

"I did," Constance said, her face guarded.

Polar Day

"Mrs. Davenport," Danny said. "I think I know what it was too. You don't have to be cryptic with me. I won't think you're crazy, believe me."

Constance let out a breath. "It was a magic book," she said. "Or at least, my grandparents believed it was magic. But my grandmother Lara hated it. She said it had gotten my grandfather killed."

"Did she say how?"

"No. Just that it happened a long time ago when she was pregnant with my father. She would never talk about it. But she said my grandfather could do magic and there was magic in his family. The book terrified her but she kept it because she said it was all she had left of my grandfather."

"Did she ever try to use the book?"

"No. She couldn't even read it. It was in Ukrainian. Ukraine was my grandfather's home. My grandmother was American and never learned his native language. None of us could read the book."

"But Jamie could?"

"Apparently. I never understood how because Robert never learned Ukrainian to my knowledge. I asked Jamie about it and he said he taught himself with Russian books and tapes he got from the library. He said the languages were similar enough that he could figure out the Ukrainian text in the book." Constance shrugged. "It didn't make much sense but what could I do but take him at his word?"

"What was it that scared you so badly?"

"Well to start, he tried to kill my daughter's hamster by setting the poor animal on fire. I thought it was some kind of terrible accident but he said he meant to do it. He said he wanted to see what would happen." Constance shook her head as if still horrified by the memory. "We had to bring the poor thing to the vet to have it euthanized. It was horrible."

"How did he start that fire?"

"We didn't know. He didn't have any matches on him when we found him watching the hamster start to burn. And we didn't have any lighters in the house; none of us have ever smoked." Constance paused again and pushed a stray strand of hair from her face. "I took him to a therapist then. I thought it was the result of the trauma of the fire. I was horrified but I tried to look at it as a clear sign that the boy desperately

146

needed help."

"What happened with the therapist?"

"After the first appointment Jamie said if I made him go back he'd treat me like he did the hamster."

"He threatened you?"

"Yes. And I don't know how to explain it, but it was as if the boy turned into some kind of devil right in front of me. His eyes looked so cold, almost lifeless, and he had a grin on his face like he was dying for the chance to make good on his threat."

"Did you go to the police?"

"I wanted to. And this is where I know I really failed. But he threatened my children too. He said if I didn't just let him go back to Fairbanks he'd get rid of all of us. He asked me if I wanted my children to meet the same fate his siblings had."

Danny remained silent as Constance stared out the window of her home. Plump tears rolled down her cheeks.

"He said he never wanted to come live with us and he didn't want a family. He said he hated his family and he hated all of us," Constance said. "Jamie said the only one of the Dzubenkos who had been worth anything was my grandfather. He had his book and that was all he wanted of his heritage."

"So you complied with his wishes? Sent him back to Fairbanks?"

"Yes." Constance dissolved into tears. "I know I was wrong. I know I should have contacted the police both here and in Fairbanks. But I was so frightened for my family. When he threatened us I was sure that he had murdered my brother. He as much as admitted it with his threats."

"Did you ever hear anything more from him?"

"No. And I'll admit that I tried to block the whole incident from my mind. As the years went on it got easier to pretend it hadn't been as bad as I'd thought back then. That I'd just been struggling with grief over my brother and the stress of having another child added to the household. And I never heard anything bad about Jamie so I just tried to let it go. I told myself that he'd been placed in a foster family that had more experience dealing with children who had been involved in trauma. I hired an investigator to check up on him a few times and the last I heard he had graduated from college and was working at the hospital there in Fairbanks. When I learned about that I convinced myself that he really had just been traumatized back then and he had turned out okay now." Constance looked at Danny with pleading eyes. "But he's not okay, is he? Has he hurt someone? Is that why you're here?"

"I can't say. I'm investigating some homicides and the fire that killed your brother and his family came to our attention."

"You think Jamie killed people?" Constance asked, begging Danny with her eyes to say no.

"I really can't say," Danny said.

"When he looked at me, I thought I understood why my grandmother had been so terrified of those books and my grandfather's magic. I saw so much evil in Jamie's eyes."

Danny nodded. While he knew the woman had been wrong to let a boy she believed to be dangerous go without a word, he also knew something about being confronted with an evil that terrified you down to your soul. He wouldn't pass judgment.

He fished a business card from his pocket and handed it to his host. "If you think of anything else that went on when Jamie was here with you, please give me a call." He covered Constance's shaking hand with his own. "I think I can understand how scared you must have been back then. I'm sorry."

Constance nodded. "Thank you," she whispered.

"I'll see myself out, ma'am."

Danny walked out to his rental car and got inside. He could see Constance at her front window, crying as she watched him. He thought of Maria Treibel and the haunted look in her eyes when she talked of Aleksei Nechayev. He remembered the fear he had felt himself when Aleksei had first bared his fangs. Constance Davenport let the curtain fall across her window and disappeared from view. Danny felt nothing but pity.

****

# Chapter 41

Danny had rarely been more relieved to see his car when he finally returned to the parking lot at the Fairbanks airport. His flight from Anchorage had been delayed four times and what was supposed to be a quick one-hour flight had turned into a tedious six-hour exercise in time wasting. He cringed as he heard the sound of his phone buzzing before he could even open the door of his car. He couldn't help but wish he had left it on airplane mode.

"Yeah?" Danny said, opening his car door and sliding behind the steering wheel.

"Are you finally back in Fairbanks?" Jack Meyer asked.

"Yes I am. Feels like I've been gone for ten years at this point. I thought my new home was going to be the Anchorage airport."

"Well you need to get back to the station. You won't believe the shit we're dealing with now."

"Considering what's been going on, if you're saying I won't believe it I'm definitely afraid to even ask what it is."

Danny cradled the phone on his shoulder as he turned out of the airport parking lot. "You need me there right now or can I go take care of my dog first? He's been alone a long time now."

"That's fine," Meyer said. "But get back here as soon as you can. Our asshole friend sent more letters to the news channels – all of them this time. It's all over on every channel and we're totally screwed."

"Why do you say that?"

"Because he warned them about his Vulcanalia bullshit and in between breathlessly sharing what that is they're all bringing on every politician they can find to talk about how the police don't have a clue who the killer is and we've wasted the whole summer twiddling our thumbs while people keep dying."

"Not that far off, is it?"

Polar Day

"Fuck off, Fitzpatrick. I don't need you agreeing with them."

"I'm not agreeing with them. But we don't have a clue what to do, do we?"

"Just go take care of your dog and then get in here."

Meyer ended the call without any further barking at Danny. Danny knew he should stop intentionally trying to get his boss' goat, as he was a good man at heart and had played a key role in saving Danny's life back in the winter, but Danny couldn't help himself. It was as easy as winding a top and significantly more entertaining.

He let out a weary sigh as he drove away from the airport and towards his apartment and undoubtedly irritated dog. He could just imagine the looks he was going to get when he left Sox again so soon after coming home. He'd have to make it up to the dog when they finally solved this case and found the lunatic who was threatening to burn down the city in less than a month. He didn't want to even consider the possibility that they may not be able to find him in time.

****

# Chapter 42

"It's about time you got your ass here," Jack Meyer said as soon as Danny walked inside the police station.

"It hasn't even been a half hour since I talked to you."

"I'm heading to the conference room. Tessa's already there. So are Rizzo and the Chief of Police. We're all just waiting for your pretty face to join the party."

Danny followed Meyer into the room and nodded at the others around the table.

"You feeling better?" he asked Tessa as he took a seat beside her. Her face was drawn and her eyes looked tired.

"A little," she said. "I can get out of bed so that's an improvement."

"So tell me about this circus with the news channels," Danny said, addressing no one in particular.

"We don't have to tell you," Jack said. "I'll show you."

Jack grabbed a remote and clicked on the television that hung from the conference room wall. Each channel was continuing to provide non-stop coverage of the killer's letters to them, the meaning of Vulcanalia, and the threat to the city of Fairbanks and its citizens. Of course, the failure of the police to apprehend the killer or even to arrest a suspect was at the forefront of every report.

"I've seen enough," Danny said. "Have you already gone over and collected their letters?"

"Yeah we've got them and forensics is going over them but we all know they're not going to find anything, don't we? Why should we get that lucky?"

"Did you get anything from Constance Davenport?" Tessa asked.

"Nothing we can use. But more anecdotal evidence that Dzubenko is batshit. He tried to kill her daughter's hamster by setting it on fire."

Polar Day

Anthony Rizzo spoke up. "Don't tell me, let me guess. They couldn't figure out how he set the hamster on fire, could they?"

"They could not," Danny answered. "She told me no one in the house smoked and to her knowledge Dzubenko didn't have a lighter. He didn't have any matches on him and there was no sign of a match in the hamster's cage. But the hamster was definitely on fire."

"What else?" Chief of Police Reggie Winston spoke for the first time since Danny had entered the room. "We need something better than a dead hamster 15 years ago."

"Actually the hamster didn't burn to death. The Davenports found the poor thing and put the fire out. But of course the animal had to be euthanized..."

"Fitzpatrick, are you purposely trying to be a pain in all of our asses?" Jack Meyer asked. "We don't give a shit about a hamster regardless of how the poor animal met its end. Don't tell me that's all you got out of your trip to Anchorage? I have to justify the expense of your flight, you know."

Danny let out a sigh. "I'm sorry. I really wasn't trying to be a pain in the ass. The hamster was a very disturbing memory for Mrs. Davenport. She put Dzubenko in therapy after that. But right after he started therapy he threatened her if she ever made him return to the therapist. He said he'd do the same thing to her kids that he had done to the hamster."

"Jesus," Chief Winston said. "So what did she do?"

"Dzubenko told her if she let him come back to Fairbanks and enter foster care he'd leave her and the rest of the family alone. He told her he hated his family and just wanted to be done with all of them. So that's what she did."

"She turned him over to foster care? That's it?" Tessa asked.

"That's it. She was terrified of him and believed his threat. She said the same thing Frank Wainscott said about him. She felt like she was looking at evil when she looked at Jamie. And she believed he had murdered her brother and the rest of his family."

"So she didn't say a word about his threats or the fact that he tried to kill an animal when she turned him over to Fairbanks?"

"No Tessa, she didn't." Danny said. "She knows it was wrong. But she was scared to death for her family. And still grieving the loss of her brother."

"But if she was that frightened how could she keep it to herself?" Jack asked. "Didn't she think she had a responsibility to alert the authorities? To warn any foster family the kid ended up with?"

The image of Aleksei Nechayev entered unbidden into Danny's mind. The conference room faded away and he could hear the roar of the Arctic wind outside the Snow Creek asylum. He could see Nechayev's fangs as he came towards him and wrapped his arms around Danny's neck...

"Danny?" Tessa asked. "Are you okay?"

Danny cleared his throat. "I'm fine." He shook off the memory. "Honestly, I felt sorry for the woman. She knows what she did was wrong. But she had four children to worry about. And Dzubenko scared the shit out of her."

"So we've got Frank Wainscott, you two," Jack said, pointing to Danny and Tessa, "and his aunt all saying that there's something not right with Jamie Dzubenko. You think the aunt would testify about him now?"

"I think she would," Danny said. "But what good would it do us at this point? It still doesn't give us any reason to arrest him now." He drummed his fingers on the desk. "But I know in my gut that he's our guy."

"You already know after what happened in Coldfoot I'm not about to dismiss your gut instincts," Jack said. "But we need more, obviously."

"And we need more fast," Winston said. "I want every available officer working this night and day until we sew up this case. And not just because we've got a PR nightmare on our hands. I don't want to see anyone else killed."

"We'll go back over everything from the night of the baseball game. Look at every second of cell phone footage and talk to everyone who was there. And talk to everyone who knew Max Fugate and Nick Torrance," Danny said.

"And go back through the surveillance camera footage from Griffin Park and the New Church of God," Tessa added.

Jack nodded. "Right. We had to have missed something the first time around. Now that we've got an idea who we might be looking for maybe we'll find it."

Winston stood up from the table. "Right now I need all of you to come with me for a press conference. I want to present a unified front and show the city we've got our best people working on this."

He left the room with the clear implication that everyone was expected to follow him. Danny glanced at Tessa, knowing she was dreading the press conference as much as he was. He knew the chief would do all the talking, but he still hated the dog and pony show that these things always turned out to be.

All Danny wanted was a drink and a cigarette. But he knew it would be a while before he could have either. He grudgingly followed Chief Winston and prepared to face the press.

# Chapter 43

Jamie couldn't suppress his smile as he sat at his desk and scrolled through the news sites on his laptop. He nibbled at the sandwich he had packed for his dinner but he was almost too excited to eat. Jamie had made a habit of taking his meal break alone in the lab. He considered it a complete waste of money to go out to restaurants and he couldn't abide the forced social interaction of the hospital cafeteria. Spending his time alone in his lab was a pleasure for Jamie. And never more so than tonight. It was pure joy to bask in the results of his efforts; putting heat on the Fairbanks police while toying with the news media.

The shrill ring of the phone on his desk interrupted his revelry. He answered it with annoyance.

"Hello."

"Jamie?"

A timid and barely audible woman's voice came through the other end of the line. Jamie recognized the voice immediately.

"This is your aunt Connie," she said.

Jamie stayed silent as he tried to calm his emotions. What the hell was this about? Why would his aunt be calling him now after all these years? After he had put the fear of God in the woman? It couldn't be good.

"Aunt Connie," Jamie finally said, clearing his throat. "What a surprise."

"I can imagine it is. How are you?"

"I'm fine. Why are you calling me? For that matter, how did you find me?"

"I hired an investigator a few years ago to check on you and find out if you were still in Fairbanks. I learned then that you worked at the hospital. So I took a chance that you still worked there and called the switchboard."

She checked on him with a private investigator? Jamie forced himself to swallow his rage.

"I can't believe you checked up on me. After all these years? Why?"

"It wasn't the first time. I wanted to keep an eye on you and make sure you were okay. I felt so terrible about everything that happened."

"Why did you feel terrible? You did what I wanted. I thought I made that clear."

"You did, you did. But you were only a kid, Jamie. And you'd been through so much."

"I was old enough to know what I wanted. And you gave that to me. I didn't want anything to do with you or anyone else in my family. And I've been just fine. Why are you calling me now?"

The silence on the other end of the line made Jamie's nerves twitch.

"Why are you calling?" he repeated.

Connie sighed audibly into the phone. "There was a detective from Fairbanks here to talk to me today. He asked about you and the fire."

"A detective? What? Why?"

"I don't really know. He just said he was looking into some old arson cases and came upon the fire that killed your family. He asked about your time here with us."

"What did you tell him?"

"The truth. I told him about the hamster and how you didn't want to be here with us. I told him you insisted we turn you over to Fairbanks so you could live with a foster family."

"And what did he say to that?"

"Nothing. He asked if I'd had contact with you since and I told him no."

"What was this detective's name?"

"Danny Fitzpatrick."

Jamie seethed. The male detective who had paid him a visit. That son of a bitch...

"You told him about the hamster?"

"I did. I thought I should. But I told him you were traumatized by the fire and not yourself at the time. Jamie, I know about the fires in

156

Fairbanks, they've been all over the news. You haven't had any part in those, have you? Please tell me you haven't hurt anyone."

"Did this Detective Fitzpatrick say that he thought I had?"

"He didn't, no. But it's not hard to put two and two together." Connie's voice dissolved into tears.

"Why are you crying?" Jamie asked, his voice brittle.

"Because I couldn't live with myself if you've killed those people. I never should have let you go on your own back then. I should have tried harder to help you."

"I didn't need help," Jamie snapped. "I still don't." He inhaled deeply and steadied his nerves. "Aunt Connie, please don't cry. I haven't done anything. This detective is desperate because the police don't have a clue who is starting these fires. He's grasping at straws just like the rest of them are."

"Are you telling me the truth? You're not just playing with me, are you?"

"Of course I'm not. Did you ever know me to play games? I was direct with you, wasn't I?"

Connie stopped crying long enough to feel the chill overtaking her body. Yes, the boy had been direct. In a way that showed there was something missing in his soul. The fear Connie had buried for years returned to her.

"Okay, I believe you." A forced and hollow laugh escaped from Connie's lips. "I'm sorry I troubled you. This detective just left me a little rattled."

"Of course he did. That's what they all want to do, isn't it? Rattle innocent people because they're too incompetent to find the guilty ones."

"I guess so. It just seemed strange he would take the time to fly here to Anchorage just to do that."

"Wasting taxpayer money by traveling. Another hallmark of the police." Jamie paused and drew in a breath. "Please don't call me again, Aunt Connie. I have my own life here. It's how I wanted it."

"I'm sorry for troubling you, Jamie..." Connie heard the line disconnect before she could finish her sentence.

Jamie's hand shook as he hung up on his aunt. How dare she interrupt his summer just when he was so close to its climax. He thought he had made it crystal clear to her way back when that he'd wanted no contact with her again.

But he knew his nosy and irritatingly stupid aunt wasn't the real reason for his anger. He had tried to shake off the visit the two detectives had made to his home. He'd kept the woman's business card and vowed to make her pay if she caused trouble for him, but he hadn't really believed their visit had been a serious threat.

Now he knew differently. The man had managed to find his family. What did he know about the fire Jamie had set to kill his parents and siblings? And how could he possibly connect it to Jamie's work now? Was it possible he knew about Jamie's heritage and his magic?

Jamie stood up from his chair and paced the lab. No, that wasn't possible. No one knew about magic in this city and state of imbeciles. None of them understood the world beyond the one they puttered around in every day, walking mindlessly through their lives.

They couldn't possibly have any real evidence against him, but the police had become a thorn in Jamie's side just the same. He walked back to his laptop and returned to the news videos that had brought him so much joy just minutes before. There was more he could do to mess with the police. It would be risky to bring attention to himself, but he knew he could manage it. He'd make Danny Fitzpatrick, Tessa Washington, and all the rest of them regret the day they got in his way. He managed a smile for the first time since his aunt had so rudely intruded on his world. This was going to be fun.

In Anchorage, Connie fidgeted with the phone in her pocket and tried unsuccessfully to stop her hands from shaking. It had been disconcerting to hear the adult voice of her nephew. In some ways, he sounded just like the brother she still missed. But his voice held none of the warmth of his father's and none of the kindness. Connie made a mistake contacting Jamie, she knew that now. Should she contact the detective and apologize to him?

Connie slumped onto her couch and stared out at the night sun, a glowing ball of fiery red and orange. She couldn't face the thought of contacting Detective Fitzpatrick and admitting her mistake. Yet another mistake in a line of so many she had made since the death of her brother. Or had it been the murder of her brother? Murder at the hands of his own son? In her heart, she knew the answer. She shuddered at the thoughts entering unbidden into her mind but she knew they carried the truth with them. Jamie's voice wasn't just lacking warmth. It was lacking humanity.

****

# Chapter 44

*August 3, 2013*

The incessant ringing of his phone on the bedside table roused Danny from his nightmares. He left the Arctic snow behind and returned to the Fairbanks summer, grabbing the phone to mercifully end the ringing without raising his head from his pillow.

"Hello?" he said.

"Danny, you need to turn on channel ten," Tessa said, not bothering with morning pleasantries.

Danny sat up in his bed. "Why?"

"Just do it. We've got one hell of a mess on our hands."

Danny got out of bed and stumbled down the hallway to his living room and television set. Sox jumped from the bed and followed dutifully behind.

"We already had that," he said. "What's happened now?"

"Jamie Dzubenko's being interviewed right now on the morning news."

Of all the things Tessa could have said, it was safe to say that was the last answer Danny would have expected. He plopped down on the couch and fumbled in the cushions for the remote he had dropped last night while watching the Mariners. He turned the television on and switched to channel ten, where he immediately saw Jamie Dzubenko's solemn face on the screen.

"I went through a terrible trauma as a child," Dzubenko said to Mick Sullivan, the reporter who sat in a chair across from him. "And now the Fairbanks police are forcing me to relive it. The deadly fires that have happened this summer already brought back horrible memories. I never dreamed our own police department would make this even worse for me."

"Goddammit," Danny said through the phone.

"I had the tv on while eating my breakfast and literally spit my coffee all over my table when they announced Dzubenko was coming up after the break," Tessa said. "The aunt obviously called him after she talked to you, Danny. That was how he started the interview. He said he received a call from his devastated aunt who was being harassed by us even though she lives in Anchorage."

"Goddammit," Danny repeated. "This goddamn son of a bitch."

Sullivan turned towards the camera with the expression of shock and disdain that was a hallmark of television journalism.

"This is the latest development in the arson murders that have plagued our city this summer. As we've already reported, we here at Channel 10 received communication allegedly from the arsonist promising more fires on August 23, the ancient feast of Vulcanalia. It's a frightening time here in Fairbanks, made more so by the belief of many that our police have not done enough to solve these crimes and keep our city safe. Now let's go back to Sarah at the news desk for more."

As Sullivan spoke, Danny watched Jamie Dzubenko, who stared mournfully at the camera. If he hadn't been paying attention he was sure he wouldn't have noticed the change. But before the cameras moved off of him, Dzubenko's lips curled into a smile. For the briefest of moments, his face turned from grief and dismay to smug satisfaction. Danny was sure of it.

"Did you see that," he asked Tessa. "The smile on that shithead's face?"

"I did. I thought maybe I was imagining it."

"You weren't."

Danny muted his television and absently scratched Sox's ears as the somber and equally disdainful face of Sarah Morgan took over his screen. The graphic behind her of flames overtaking a building had the question "Are police doing enough to keep us safe?" superimposed over the image.

"I called Jack before I called you," Tessa said. "Needless to say, he wants us at the station immediately if not sooner."

"Right. Can't say I'm looking forward to watching the whole interview when I get there. I already want to get my hands on this asshole and wipe that smirk off his face. God damn the aunt. I should have known she'd cave. It was clear she wasn't the strongest person in the world already. I shouldn't have left her alone."

"What choice did you have? What were you supposed to do? Move in with her? This isn't your fault."

"Well whether it is or isn't, there's one thing that's not up for debate."

"What's that?"

"This is going to be one hell of a day at work."

\*\*\*\*

Julie Flanders

# Chapter 45

"I was stunned when my aunt Constance called me last night and said a police detective from Fairbanks had been to her house to question her. This detective had nearly frightened her to death. Of course, she'd heard about the fires here. When the detective first contacted her she was terrified that I had been killed in one of them."

Danny, Tessa, Jack, Anthony Rizzo and Chief Winston sat around the table in the conference room re-watching Jamie Dzubenko's star-making interview with Mick Sullivan. Since the interview had first aired, Dzubenko was now making the rounds of every television and radio station in town and reportedly fielding requests from the national cable news networks as well.

"You have a traumatic history with fire," Mick Sullivan said with appropriate solemnity. "Can you tell us about that?"

Jamie inhaled and closed his eyes as if preparing himself for what he knew was going to be a painful moment.

"Yes, of course. My family home here in Fairbanks burned down in 1996 when I was twelve. My parents and siblings didn't make it out of the house alive. I was the only survivor." Jamie paused and let out a deep breath. "I went to live with my aunt Constance in Anchorage but I was a traumatized child and things didn't go well. She was my closest living relative but I barely knew her since she'd moved to Anchorage when I was very young. And I missed my family and my home. I really wanted to come back to Fairbanks...."

"What happened? Did you end up staying in Anchorage?"

Jamie shook his head. "No. And my behavior with my aunt is not something I'm proud of today, I know I hurt her and she was trying to do her best by taking me in. But I insisted that I didn't want to live with her and I wanted to come back here instead. I felt like I could somehow be close to my parents and siblings here at home. So I went into foster

163

care and lived with some wonderful families before striking out on my own when I turned 18 and aged out of the system."

"Before you heard from your aunt, did you have contact with the police yourself?"

"I did. Two detectives who said they were investigating the fires came to visit me a few weeks ago. I couldn't understand at all why they visited me and told them so. I certainly never imagined they'd then go to my aunt and upset her as well."

"Did they tell you why they visited you?"

"They said they were looking into unsolved arson cases and came upon my family's case from the '90s. I have no idea why they thought that could possibly have anything to do with the terrible killings in our city this year."

"Have you ever had any trouble with the police?"

"You mean have I been arrested? No, never. I've had a few speeding tickets but I didn't realize that could make someone suspect me of arson and murder."

"You mentioned that you were in foster care. I imagine those years were difficult."

"Well of course they were, but mostly because I missed my family so much. I have no complaints about the families I lived with. I can't say I developed strong relationships with any of them but at that point I really just wanted to keep to myself. To me that was what I needed to do to survive."

"Which is exactly what you've done?"

"Yes, it's what I've done. It's been a long road, but I'm doing well now. I've worked in the lab at Fairbanks General for more than ten years. I love science and the lab suits me perfectly. I don't know if this is because of the trauma of my past but I'm a loner, I can't deny that. I enjoy working on my own. But I also enjoy knowing I'm helping with the care of our patients at the hospital."

"Christ, could he lay it on any thicker?" Danny asked, pressing the pause button on the interview. "Hard to imagine anyone is as perfect as this guy is pretending to be."

"The thing is he's telling the truth," Chief Winston said. "At least in terms of the facts. He has no record, adult or juvenile. And his foster care records show no red flags. He lived with three different families and none of them reported any threatening behavior or anything close to what the aunt described to you. They all said he was a loner, but that's the extent of it. We really don't have anything on this guy and we look like a bunch of clowns right now."

"You mean I look like a clown," Danny said. "I'm the one who found his old case and the one who went to Anchorage."

"You didn't do it on your own," Jack said. "Far be it from me to lay waste to your martyr complex but we all agreed it was a lead worth pursuing."

Anthony Rizzo played with the laptop in front of him and frowned. "Fairbanks Fires is a trending topic on Twitter now," he said, glancing up from the screen towards his colleagues. "Alaska hasn't had this much national attention since the country was introduced to Sarah Palin."

"Well you can bet your ass the news channels will have reporters camped out here before the day is out," Jack said, wiping beads of sweat from his brow.

The summer heatwave had only intensified as the calendar had turned over to August, bringing the tensions surrounding the fires to a boil.

"We can't handle this on our own now. I'm bringing in the FBI," the chief said. "We've got no defense for the accusations that we're not doing enough to find the arsonist. We can't point to any progress and our only lead just made fools out of us in front of the whole city. And soon enough the whole damn country."

"If anything, this makes him seem even guiltier to me," Tessa said. "He's shrewd. Would an innocent person really think to go on television immediately if they found out they were being investigated? Wouldn't they be frightened and freaked out instead? Instead he sought out attention. I think he's enjoying this."

"I don't see that when I watch him," Chief Winston said.

"All due respect, sir," Danny said. "But I think that's because you haven't met him. Tessa and I have. He's not the angel he's presenting himself as."

"That may very well be the case. But as the man has made clear to the world, we have no evidence against him. People have been burning to death in our city for three months now and we have no evidence against anyone! So all due respect to you as well, detective, but this isn't up for discussion. I'm handing the case over to the FBI Violent Crime unit. They're coming in from the Anchorage office and we'll hold a press conference ASAP to announce that they are now going to be the point people on this case and we'll be offering them our full cooperation. If the son of a bitch who is sending out the letters is telling the truth, we've only got a little more than a week before he starts burning the whole damn city for his Vulcan festival or whatever the hell it is. We should have called in the FBI before this got so far out of hand."

Danny started to protest, but stopped himself when he noticed Jack drawing a finger across his throat to silently tell Danny to be quiet. He gave an involuntary shiver. He knew perfectly well the gesture was a universal sign to shut up and Jack only meant it as such, but Danny could never see it again without thinking of Caroline's murder and the fact that her throat had literally been sliced right in front of him. That memory quieted him as much as, or perhaps more, than Jack's unfortunate choice of gestures.

Chief Winston glanced around the table as if daring anyone to argue with him. Met with silence, he stood up and walked towards the door.

"We're clear then," he said. "Jack, I'll want you in on the press conference. The rest of you, I'll let you know when the special agents arrive so you can give them whatever information they need to get started."

****

# Chapter 46

Danny scowled as he looked towards the station conference room and watched Jack and Chief Winston meeting with the FBI Special Agents who were now in charge of his case. The woman was tall and slender, with straight red hair cut in a chin length bob. She wore glasses and fiddled with the frames repeatedly while reading files on her laptop. The man was shorter than the woman and also much heavier. His black hair was nearly as thick and unruly as the mop Danny carried on top of his head. He was more animated than his colleague, gesturing with his hands as he talked to Winston with an obvious sense of urgency. Despite their differences in appearance and manner the two agents followed the same dress code. They wore perfectly tailored conservative suits, the man's grey and the woman's navy blue. Both seemed completely impervious to the stifling heat that had worsened with each passing day.

Danny had met the agents earlier in the day but had already forgotten their names. Or perhaps he had purposely chosen to not remember them. He would be happy to pretend they didn't exist.

"What are their names again?" he asked Tessa, who sat across from him at her own desk.

"Who?"

"Our special agent friends."

"Holly Thompson and John Castillo. Why?"

"No reason. I just couldn't remember." Danny was quiet as he continued to watch the agents. "They're not going to solve anything though," he finally said. "How are they supposed to find anything in such a short amount of time? We already know who the killer is but they won't listen to us."

"They can't listen to us."

"They can't? They won't. There's a difference."

## Polar Day

Tessa slammed her hand on her desk in frustration. "And just what do you expect them or any of the rest of us to do? You watched the same circus we did this morning."

"So we should be cowed by the media? Let them decide who we can investigate?"

"Don't put words in my mouth. And don't try to make me into some kind of damn fool." Tessa turned her laptop towards Danny and pointed at the screen. "Our friend Dzubenko is live on CNN right now talking about police harassment. He's got us over a barrel and all the righteous indignation you can muster isn't going to change that."

"I'm sorry," Danny said. "It's just so damn frustrating."

"You think I'm not frustrated? I am, trust me. And not just because I agree with you about Dzubenko." She glared at the interview unfolding on the screen in front of her. "You know how long I've lived in Fairbanks? For as long as I can remember, no one outside of Alaska has ever given a shit what happens here in our city. Hell most of the time no one else in the state gives a damn. If it doesn't happen in Anchorage or Juneau it's not news. The only time I can think of, that we got any kind of publicity, was when you uncovered Nechayev. But now we've got everybody in America weighing in on our department and our city and talking about how corrupt and incompetent we supposedly are. All because of some psychopathic piece of shit that you and I both know is guilty." Tessa slammed her laptop closed. "Don't talk to me about being frustrated, Danny."

Danny had nothing to say in response. He got up from his chair and headed towards the front door of the building. "I need a cigarette," he said over his shoulder.

As he walked out onto the sidewalk, Danny was hit simultaneously by the glare of the afternoon sun and the oppressive heat which refused to give the city a break. He wondered if there was any weather extreme this god-forsaken city was immune from. When he'd come here and suffered through his first Alaskan winter, he had found some comfort in the fact that he was at least free of the heat and humidity that blanketed Chicago throughout the summer months. But now it seemed the heat and humidity had followed him.

He lit his cigarette and inhaled a welcome blast of nicotine. He savored the smoke in his mouth before slowly blowing it out and watching it disappear into the oppressive air around him. He'd needed the calming influence of the cigarette before he did what he'd really come outside to do.

Reaching into this pocket, Danny withdrew his phone and punched in the number before he had a chance to change his mind. He heard the voice that filled his nightmares after only two rings.

"Hello, Detective Fitzpatrick. Nice to hear from you," Aleksei said.

"I need your help."

"Interesting. Remind me again why I should give it to you."

Danny ignored the remark. "Have you still been following the news?"

"You mean the news about your colossal screw-up there? I did see some of Jamie Dzubenko's interviews. Terrible the way you and your fellow officers harassed that man and his poor aunt."

"Fuck off, Nechayev."

Aleksei chuckled. "Again I need to ask why I should help you. I would think you'd at least try to be pleasant instead of insulting me with vulgar profanity. I detest that sort of language."

"We didn't harass Dzubenko and you know that. He's the guy who set the fires and killed all those people. There's no doubt in my mind."

"I agree with you. I also don't care. What makes you think this concerns me?"

"Because I know Dzubenko's ancestor tried to kill you. I thought helping me take him down would be a chance for you to even the score."

"I already did that when I arranged for Vasyl Dzubenko to be killed before he could finish killing me. My score was settled a long time ago. And I won. Your complete inability to handle your own Dzubenko witch is of no consequence to me. If anything, I'm amused by it. Your incompetence has provided me with a great deal of entertainment over the past few months."

"Well then how about helping me out in exchange for all that free entertainment? Or just because you owe me."

"I owe you? For what?"

"I broke you out of your rut, remember? I opened up a new life for you by exposing your games up in the Arctic. You're the one who told me you were grateful to me for that."

"Yes. And I allowed you to live. That was my way of saying thank you. I told you that as well."

"Alright then. How about just doing it because you can enjoy the fact that I've been reduced to begging you for help? That has to bring you some satisfaction."

"It does, you're right about that." Aleksei paused for so long that Danny wondered if the connection had been lost. "What do you want from me?" he finally asked.

"I want to know about the witchcraft that Jamie and his family possess. Can I learn it?"

"What?" Aleksei asked, genuinely surprised by the question.

"You heard me. Can I learn this witchcraft so I can use it against Dzubenko?"

Danny bristled at the sound of Aleksei's laughter on the other end of the line.

"You really do have a high opinion of yourself, don't you?"

"Just answer my goddamn question!"

"Alright, alright. No, you can't learn this. Witches are born with their power. So unless you come from a long line of Fitzpatrick witches and you're just not aware of it, you're out of luck. Didn't I already tell you this when we first chatted?" Aleksei chuckled again. "Let me ask you something though. If you could learn this, do you honestly think you could do it in time to stop Dzubenko? From what I read in the News-Miner, your boy has big plans for Vulcanalia on August 23. You think you can learn centuries, or more accurately, millennia, of witchcraft in one week?"

"Fair enough. If I can't learn it, are there other witches here in Alaska who know it? Surely Dzubenko's not the only one."

"How would I know?"

"How many decades did you live here, Nechayev? You think I'm stupid? That I believe a witch nearly succeeded in killing you and you never bothered to find out if you faced a threat from anyone else? You know and don't try to pretend otherwise."

"To my knowledge," Aleksei said, "there were no other witches in Alaska who practiced black magic. Dzubenko was it as far as I could determine and as the decades passed I honestly stopped worrying about it. But I never got any indication that any new witches had moved into the state."

"You said black magic. Is there some other kind of magic?"

"Of course. There's magic that is used for good instead of evil. Or at least what you would consider evil. There was a line of witches in Fairbanks who were known for their use of natural magic. Silly things like curing illnesses or controlling the weather to help farmers, that sort of nonsense. Dzubenko had this kind of magic too, though. The truly powerful witches have both."

"So these witches in Fairbanks aren't as powerful as the Dzubenkos?"

"I have no idea. They could be and they've just chosen not to use their black magic."

"Could they stop Dzubenko now?"

"Again I have no idea. It's been a long time since I heard anything about this family. But my first thought is that if they could stop him, they would have tried by now. They must be aware of his power. Supernatural beings like me are always attuned to others of our kind."

"Why didn't they come after you then?"

"Because they weren't stupid. I'm sure word of what I did to Vasyl Dzubenko spread quickly. Even supernatural beings don't take on fights they can't win."

Danny rolled his eyes at Aleksei's arrogance. Some things never changed.

"Who are they then? How can I find them?"

"Their name was Locklear. The last I heard the only Locklear left was running a new age Wiccan shop in Fairbanks. I never knew her first name."

"What was the name of the shop?"

"Do I have to take you by the hand and do everything for you? I don't know the name. That's something I would expect an officer of the law to be able to find out on his own."

"Alright."

"You'll keep me abreast of what happens, right?" Aleksei asked. "Have fun, detective."

Danny ended the call without responding. He knew the name Locklear rang a bell, and suddenly remembered searching for and finding a magic store in Fairbanks when he'd first tried pursuing a supernatural line of investigation in this case. Locklear's Metaphysical Mementos was the store. This had to be the Wiccan shop Aleksei mentioned. He lit another cigarette and leaned against the wall of the station as he searched google to quickly find the store again. Madeline Locklear was listed as the owner and manager. For once, something came easily. He wasn't foolish enough to think that meant the lead would pan out, but at least it was a start. At least it was something.

He returned the phone to his pocket and pulled out his car keys in its place. He went to his car without going back inside to talk to Tessa or Jack. If they wanted him, they could call him. This visit to Madeline Locklear was something he needed to do on his own.

****

# Chapter 47

Bells jingled as Danny walked into the dimly-lit magic store. Seeing no one at the counter, he glanced around at the store shelves, taking in the rows of candles, crystals, gemstones and tarot cards. The shop smelled of incense, taking Danny back to a girl he dated in high school who used incense to hide the marijuana smell that permeated her bedroom from her parents. He was certain the incense had a different use here, and to his surprise he found the aroma calming. Perhaps that was the point.

His thoughts were interrupted by a woman who came through a curtain of beads that apparently separated the back office from the front of the store. She was tall and heavyset, her ample bust draped with gold chains and a necklace with a large pentagram pendant. Her dark brown hair was drawn into a loose bun at the back of her head, and she watched Danny with clearly suspicious brown eyes.

"May I help you?" she asked.

"Are you Madeline Locklear?"

"I am. And you are?"

Danny removed his badge from his belt and showed it to Locklear. "I'm Detective Danny Fitzpatrick. Fairbanks PD."

Madeline took an involuntary step back, something Danny had long been used to. Most people did when they found the police at their door. A puzzled and guarded expression replaced the suspicion on her face.

"Is there something I can help you with?" Madeline asked.

"I'm here to talk about the fires that have been happening in our city this summer. I'm sure you've heard about them."

Madeline's hand went to her chest and she fingered the pendant. "I've heard of them, of course. But I can't imagine what you'd want to talk to me about."

"Have you heard of me before, Ms. Locklear? Do you recognize me?"

Madeline started to shake her head no, until a glimmer of recognition passed over her face. "You're the detective who found those women in the Arctic."

"Right. That's me. But I want to talk about the man who kidnapped and killed those women, Aleksei Nechayev. Have you ever met him?"

"Met him? No. Why do you ask?"

"Do you know anything about him? Maybe you've heard something unusual about him?"

Madeline took another step backwards. "I don't know anything about that man. I don't understand what this is about."

Danny let out a breath. "I'll tell you what it's about. But first let me say that I think you're lying to me. I think you do know something about Aleksei Nechayev. I think you know he wasn't just an ordinary man who also happened to be a psychotic killer."

Madeline shook her head. "Detective, I…"

"Let me put it to you this way. I know there's something unusual about Aleksei Nechayev. There's something I know about him that if I told most people they'd think I needed a mental health evaluation. In fact they'd probably have me committed. But I don't think you're one of those people. I think you know the same thing I know about him." Danny paused and locked his own brown eyes with Madeline Lockhart's. "I know that some of the things most people think are fantasy aren't that at all. I know that some of the things most people believe to be merely the stuff of legends and horror movies are real. And I think you know that too, Ms. Locklear."

Madeline pursed her lips. Her hands moved from her chest to the counter in front of her. "Why don't you come in the back with me," she said.

Danny followed her through the strands of beads to an office nearly filled to capacity with unopened boxes of items that would replenish the magic supplies in the store whenever they were sold. A desk and an old and worn leather chair stood in the middle of the towers of boxes. An open laptop sat in the center of the desk, surrounded by piles of books.

Madeline briefly disappeared into another room and returned moments later with a beat up folding chair. She unfolded it next to the desk.

"Have a seat," she said, as she sat down herself at her desk. Her fingers once again caressed the pendant at her chest. "What is it you want to talk to me about?"

"You're a witch, aren't you?" Danny asked.

"Excuse me?"

"You heard me."

"I practice the Wiccan religion if that's what you mean."

"It isn't. I understand that's the point of your store here. Wiccan supplies. I'm sure you get a lot of school girls coming in here buying lockets and trinkets to make some boy love them."

"That's not what Wicca is about," Madeline said, clearly insulted.

Danny held up his hand. "Whatever. I'm not interested in discussing religion with you. Yours or anyone else's. Truth be told I don't have much use for any of them. I want to talk about witchcraft. The real thing. Not this New Age spirituality shit you're peddling out front."

Madeline let out another long sigh. "Alright. What do you want to know?"

"How powerful are you?"

"I don't know how to answer that. I have powers but..."

"The person I believe is setting these fires is a witch. I want to know if you're as powerful as he is."

"I'm not," Madeline said definitely.

"You didn't even take time to think about it. How do you know?"

"Because I've suspected all summer that black magic was behind the fires. I didn't want to believe it but as it went on it was the only thing that made sense."

"I agree. But that doesn't answer my question."

"I know what kind of power it takes to practice magic that evil and ancient. And I know I don't have it."

"Then what kind of power do you have? What kind of magic can you do?"

"My magic is all natural. Everything I do is intended for good. I merely help people if I can, that's all."

"Well I'm asking you to help me. If I brought you to this person, could you stop him? Could you prevent him from starting any more fires?"

Madeline shook her head. "No. I'm telling you, I don't have that kind of power. I can perform protection spells and healing rituals but I can't do anything against black magic this strong."

"Healing rituals? What are you, like a shaman of some kind?"

"I'm a witch, period. But yes, there are similarities between my magic and that of a shaman."

"That crap out there that you sell…"

"It's not crap!"

Danny held up his hand. "Sorry. The supplies you sell. Do any of them do a damn thing?"

"They do if you believe in their power."

"So if I believe in them, they might be able to help me take this guy out?"

"Detective I've already told you, I don't have anything magical that can 'take out' a witch as powerful as this man you're talking about. Black magic is more powerful. The spells this witch is using are more powerful than anything in my arsenal."

"What about other witches? Are there any around that could take him out?"

"Not that I'm aware of. I'm one of the few true witches in Alaska as far as I know. The only one in Fairbanks. Or at least I thought I was until this summer. I've never known of a witch with this kind of power before. This is the sort of thing you only read about in the history books."

"When you say true you mean witches who can actually do something besides lighting candles and chanting, right?"

"Right."

"Alright, so let's get back to your supplies. Can you sell me something that can at least protect me against this witch? Make it so he can't set me on fire?"

"I can put a protection spell on an amulet for you. I can't promise it will stop him but I'll do my best."

"I'm up for anything. Give it your best shot."

"Wait here."

Madeline disappeared through the beads and returned to the front of the store.

Danny longed for a cigarette and briefly wondered if Madeline would mind if he smoked in her office. He knew that lighting up probably wasn't a good idea so he put his nicotine craving out of his mind. He glanced around at the seemingly endless rows of boxes and noticed a black suitcase and matching carry-on bag in the corner of the room. Both looked as if they were packed to the gills. Apparently Madeline was getting ready for a trip.

"I've got the amulet for you," Madeline said, returning to her desk chair.

She placed a silver and green circular medallion on the desk in front of Danny.

"This is the mohammeden magic circle. It's ancient magic to protect you from harm. I put an extra spell on it for you. Just keep it on your person."

Danny looked down at the medallion and picked it up. He fingered it, not believing for one second that it could protect him from fire or anything else.

"You know, it's a shame I didn't know about these circles a few years ago. I could have gotten one for my wife."

"Your wife was harmed?"

"Yeah she was harmed. She was murdered, actually." Danny looked across the desk at Madeline. "You really believe something like this could have saved her? Could it have stopped a psycho from slitting her throat?"

Madeline shook her head. "I can't say for sure. Nothing I do is a guarantee. I'm very sorry for your loss though."

Danny nodded and put the medallion in his pocket. "Thank you," he said. "And I'm sorry for acting like a jackass. I came here to ask for your help and you're doing what you can. I appreciate that. What do I owe you for the amulet?"

"You don't owe me anything. It's on me. I hope it will help you."

"You and me both." Danny gestured towards the luggage he had noticed earlier. "Are you going on a trip?" he asked.

"Yes," Madeline said. "It wasn't exactly planned, but…"

"But what?"

"I want to get out of Fairbanks."

"Because of the fires?"

"Yes. I'm closing the store for the rest of the month and going to visit a friend in Arizona."

"You've heard about the Vulcanalia threats, obviously."

"I've seen the news, yes. It's very frightening."

"That it is." Danny stood up from his chair and moved to the curtain of beads that led back to the store. "I don't blame you a bit," he said. "I think a lot of people will be doing the same thing if they can."

Madeline followed Danny out into her store. "Detective, may I ask you, what is your plan for stopping this man you believe is setting the fires?"

Danny sighed. "Honestly, I couldn't tell you. I came here on the miniscule chance that you could help me find a witch who could stop him."

"How did you know that I'm a real witch?"

"Well, you have a wiccan supply store so..."

"Don't lie to me."

"I don't know what you're talking about."

"It was the vampire, wasn't it?"

"Excuse me?"

Madeline met Danny's eyes. "You said it yourself. You and I both know things that others don't. I know about Aleksei Nechayev. He obviously knew about me as well."

"I can't reveal my sources, Ms. Locklear."

Seemingly satisfied and knowing she was right, Madeline nodded. "So your plan for finding another witch didn't work. What's next?"

Danny shook his head and let out a breath. "I'll just have to deal with him myself."

"Deal with him?"

Now it was Danny who met Madeline's gaze. "Kill him. If I have to, that is. He may be powerful but I doubt he's more powerful than a bullet. If magic can't stop him I'll stop him my way."

Madeline didn't flinch. "Good luck then. And blessed be."

Danny nodded and walked out of the store into the afternoon sun. As he returned to his car, he reached into his pocket and fingered the amulet.

## Julie Flanders

\*\*\*\*

# Chapter 48
*August 16, 2013*

"One week," Jack said, sitting down on the chair across from Danny and Tessa's desks. "One measly week before some lunatic sets this whole city on fire."

Danny gestured towards the conference room where the FBI agents John Castillo and Holly Thompson were once again in deep conversation with Chief Winston. "What do the special agents in charge have to say? Did they solve the case yet?"

"Castillo told me this morning that they've got a lead on a serial arsonist from Anchorage who reportedly moved here to Fairbanks last spring. They're looking for him. They've sent out notices to the press asking for the public's help in tracking him down."

Tessa snorted. "I bet whoever this guy is; he's never set foot in Fairbanks. This is just a stalling tactic to convince the public and the media that they've made progress where we didn't."

"I wouldn't bet against you on that," Jack said.

Danny turned his laptop so that it was facing both Jack and Tessa. "There might not be many people left in the city to convince pretty soon. Look at this."

A breathless young female news reporter stood outside the main entrance of the Fairbanks airport. Her long blonde hair blew around her face as she discussed the scene unfolding behind her.

"Rob," she said to the anchor back at the studio, "as you can see the airport is as crowded as it's ever been. Airport personnel tell me this is far more crowded than even the day before Thanksgiving. Obviously lots of Fairbanks residents have decided to leave the city."

As the reporter talked, a steady stream of people walked behind her pulling luggage and carrying duffle bags. Many parents grasped the hands of older children while pushing younger ones in front of them in strollers. Very few of the people filing past onscreen were talking and there were no smiles to be found among the crowd. The scene was one of tension and mounting fear.

Rob the anchor's voice talked over the scene. "Hilary, have these folks said why they are leaving our city? Is it the fire threat that has them seeking a change of scenery?"

"Yes it is, Rob," Hilary said. "Everyone I've talked to has said the same thing. They simply don't feel comfortable remaining in Fairbanks until this threat has passed. They've all said they feel lucky they have somewhere else to go and the means to get there."

"Nothing like stating the obvious," Danny said. "Do you think they're leaving because someone is about the burn the city down? Gee, I wonder."

"I wonder if there are any flights left at this point," Tessa said.

She booted up her own laptop and moved her fingers quickly over the keyboard. "Trying to get a reservation for tomorrow and there's nothing. Nothing the next day either. No seats on any flight out of Fairbanks." She typed some more. "No, wait. Tomorrow there are two seats left on a midnight flight from Fairbanks to Cleveland. Three stops and 16 hours of travel time all told. In ten minutes I bet this one will be snatched up too."

"People who can't fly are going to start driving out," Jack said. "I think we're going to need to put an evacuation plan in place."

"Do you think the Chief will let the police handle that or will the agents be managing that as well?" Danny asked.

Jack rolled his eyes. "I think you know the answer to that. I hardly think two FBI agents are going to handle a city-wide evacuation. Although if it comes to that I would imagine the governor will want to involve the National Guard to keep order."

Danny stood up from his desk and stretched. "Well, I can see they don't need me right now so I'm taking off."

"And doing what?" Jack asked.

"Just following up on some ideas I had before the FBI took the case away from us."

"You're not going after Dzubenko, are you?"

"Now why would I harass an innocent man, Captain?"

"Fitzpatrick, I swear to God if you go off on some goose chase again…"

"That would be terrible, wouldn't it? Going off on a wild goose chase and catching a murderer before he could kill more people? Why would a cop want to do that?"

"God damn your smartass mouth. You know damn well I agree with you about Dzubenko but you also know our hands are tied."

"I do know that. And I'm not doing anything to further harm poor Mr. Dzubenko. Honestly, I'm just going out to work off some steam. I can't stand sitting around here watching those agents screw around with our case. I just want to get out and think for a while. Clear my head and try to figure out what we've been missing all summer."

"Fair enough," Jack said. "But keep your goddamn phone turned on."

"Of course. That goes without saying."

Jack glanced at Tessa and rolled his eyes as he watched Danny leave the station and head to his car.

****

# Chapter 49

One week. After all these years of preparation, that's all the time that was left now. One week.

Jamie found it difficult to harness his excitement, but he knew he needed to remain calm. Not only to make sure he didn't have any last minute mistakes, but also to contain his energy. He was going to need all of it to finish his plans.

Ever since he'd discovered his power as a child and learned that his family had done nothing to nurture or encourage it, and instead they'd done everything they could to keep him from it, he'd hated all of them and hated the city that they called home. He hated the families in his neighborhood, the idiotic children he'd been forced to play with, the moronic teachers he'd had to pretend to respect. As soon as he honed his power enough to dispose of his family he'd known that one day he would dispose of the whole city.

In all the years he'd studied and worked in Fairbanks he'd never once thought that perhaps he should go back on his goal and let the city continue to go on with business as usual around him. He had no personal grudge against most of the people in the city, but his quest was about much more than grudges. As soon as he'd learned of Vulcan, the ancient god of fire, he'd realized that Vulcan was the origin of the power that coursed through him. He knew he needed to go back to the ancient ways of honoring Vulcan in order to maintain the power of his magic and his fire. His own family hadn't been respectful of the magic that made them special and different than everyone else. They'd thrown away their own history. He had no intention of making that mistake.

Once he conquered Fairbanks through Vulcanalia he had no doubt that Vulcan would shower him with even more power and privilege. He couldn't wait to find out what that new power would be and where it would take him.

But first he needed to continue the plan he had started on decades earlier. He closed his eyes and envisioned the buildings he planned to burn to kick off the festival. Thanks to his practice over the summer he knew he would have no problem setting them on fire without even leaving his apartment.

At 12:01 on August twenty-third the feast of Vulcanalia would begin. And Jamie would set the first building ablaze.

****

# Chapter 50

Danny stood at the firing range and stared at the silhouette target in front of him, a figure of a man with a red X where his heart would be. He had already put on his headphones and safety goggles and he stood with his feet shoulder-width apart, his left foot a step in front of his right. He aimed the gun at the red X and caressed the trigger with his finger. He couldn't fire the gun.

Although Danny had his police issued nine-millimeter service pistol with him at all times, he had yet to fire it since coming to Fairbanks. It had been a long time since he'd actually fired a weapon. Sometimes it felt like a lifetime ago. Other times it seemed as if just seconds had passed.

Danny had last fired a gun when he'd killed his wife's murderer back in Chicago. He'd had the gun trained on his former partner as the man held a knife to Caroline's throat, but he hadn't been able to fire. He'd been frozen with fear and terrified that his former partner would slit his wife's throat the second Danny fired the pistol. As a result, Caroline was dead, murdered so close to Danny that her blood had soaked through his clothes to coat his skin in red. Danny had finally fired his gun at his partner and hit his target squarely in his heart. But not before the man had sliced his knife across Caroline's neck, severing her carotid artery and leaving Danny alone in a world he now hated.

For a time, Danny had been sure he'd never work as a cop again. He hadn't particularly cared if he worked, or lived, at all. But the practicalities of life had won out in the end and he'd taken up a gun and a badge here in his new home of Fairbanks. And now he knew he had to be ready to fire his gun again.

He closed his eyes and inhaled slowly, foolishly wishing that smoking was allowed at the range. When he opened his eyes, he zeroed in on his target and finally pulled the trigger. His shot barely found the outside edge of the silhouette's shoulder. He fired six times in quick succession, emptying the revolver's magazine, and never came close to his target.

Cursing himself and his memories, Danny reloaded the magazine and prepared for another round. He hoped he'd find a way to stop Jamie Dzubenko without shooting him, but he had a feeling that wouldn't be possible. And if he again found himself face to face with a murderer, he had no intention of hesitating this time.

Danny channeled the anger he felt over the politicians and police administrators handing the Dzubenko case over to the FBI onto the target and came much closer to the red X with his next round of bullets. He thought of the scene he'd witnessed on Chestnut Street as he'd driven to the range from the station. A huddle of frightened people clustered around the minister of Fairbanks Baptist Church praying for God to save them from the fires. Across the street, a man paced back and forth on the corner carrying a sign that said "Repent before you burn!" The savvy owner of the hardware store on Meyers Road had stocked up on fire extinguishers right after the baseball game fire and now sold them at four times their regular price.

Danny hadn't even been able to cross the bridge at Walnut Street because the traffic was too backed up with cars heading out of town. It reminded Danny of the scenes he'd watched on the television; news of cities faced with an impending hurricane. In those situations, everyone with the means to evacuate the area did. The rest were forced to hunker down and hope they made it through the crisis with their lives and their homes intact. This was what faced the residents of Fairbanks now as the madman's August 23 date loomed large on the calendar. The city was collapsing without a single fire being set.

After pulling his target back to him and replacing the battered silhouette on the line with a clean one, Danny once again reloaded the magazine of his gun. He got into his firing stance and set his sights on the new target. Before he knew it, the dark silhouette was replaced with the tall and imposing figure of Aleksei Nechayev. The head took on his blond hair and smug smile and his soulless blue eyes stared back at Danny from the end of the range.

Danny fired his gun and hit the red X on his first shot.

\*\*\*\*

# Chapter 51

"Detective Fitzpatrick? This is Melissa Harris."

Danny stared at the unfamiliar number on his phone and tried to remember if he'd ever met a Melissa Harris. Was this a woman he'd met in a bar? He hoped not. The voice sounded like that of a teenage girl. Surely he hadn't ever sunk that low.

"I'm sorry. Do I know you?" he asked.

"I talked to you at the baseball game. After the fire."

Danny jogged his memory and finally placed the voice on the other end of the line. She sounded like a teenage girl because she was. And she had witnessed the death of Nick Torrance after she and her boyfriend had gone into the woods to make out during the baseball game.

"Of course, I remember you now, Melissa. What can I do for you?"

"You gave us your business card at the game. That's how I got your number."

"I remember," Danny said.

He could tell that whatever the girl was calling about made her very nervous. Not that he could blame her considering how she and Danny had met. He decided against ending the silence on the line and trying to push her to talk. She had made the call and would get to the reason in her own time.

"I hope it's okay that I'm calling you," she said.

"It is."

Finally, the silence appeared to be enough for her. "I wanted to talk to you about how Will and I heard that chanting when that man..." she paused again. "When that man was killed," she finally said.

"What about it? Did you hear it again?"

"No. But you know the man who has been on the news a lot?

187

Jamie Dzubenko?"

Danny sat up straight in his chair. "Yes. What about him?"

"When I heard him talking, I thought it was the same voice as the one we heard chanting."

"Really? You think so?"

"Yeah. I listened to him a bunch of times now. I think it's the same voice. Will agrees with me."

The sound of Danny's heart thumping in his chest drowned out all of the other noise in the police station.

"This is really helpful. Can you and Will talk to your parents about coming in and making a statement for us?"

"No, no, I can't," Melissa said, alarm in her voice. "My mom doesn't even know I'm calling you. I don't want to tell her. She told me she didn't want me to talk to the police anymore after we talked to you at the park. She said she was scared to have me involved in the case and we had already helped you as much as we could."

"This is very important, Melissa."

"I know but I can't tell my parents. They're so freaked out by the fires and the fact that Will and I were there at the game. They'll freak!"

"What about Will? How about if the two of you come in together with your parents. We can talk as a group."

"Will's not even here. He and his family went to Juneau last week. We're all leaving Fairbanks until the fires stop. Everyone is!" Melissa paused and tried unsuccessfully to steady her voice. "Will can't come in. And I can't either. I never should have even called you!"

"Melissa, calm down," Danny said. "We can figure something out here. I really need your help on this. People are in danger."

"I know and I'm sorry but I can't help. I thought if I just called you…"

"You're a smart girl. You knew that wouldn't be enough. I think you want to help but you don't want to upset your parents. That's understandable. But if I can just talk to you all together…"

"No! I already told you, you can't. I shouldn't have called. I'm sorry."

"Melissa!"

Danny heard the line go dead and tossed his phone on his desk just as Tessa walked up behind him.

"What's wrong?" she asked.

"You remember those kids who were out in the woods when the fire started at the baseball game?"

"Sure. The ones who told us they heard chanting?"

"Exactly. The girl just called me up and said she recognized Jamie Dzubenko's voice when she heard him on television. She's certain it's the same voice she heard chanting that night. The boy is too."

"They are?" Tessa asked, unable to keep the excitement from her voice. "So we've finally got something on him?"

"Not so fast. The boy and his family left town last week so he's not around for us to talk to. And the girl's parents don't want her to have anything more to do with the case or with us. They're terrified and so is she. She said she just thought she could help by calling me. She says she can't let her parents know she called and can't talk to us again."

"Well, she can and she will. These are murders we're talking about!"

"You think I don't know that? But what the hell are we supposed to do? We can't seize a kid and bring her down here to the station."

"No, but we can go out to the house. We can meet with her and her parents together and make them understand that lives are at stake here and we need Melissa to make a statement."

Danny nodded. "True enough. Let's go pay the Harris family a visit." He stood up from his desk and pointed towards Jack Meyer's office. "Should we let the boss know what we're up to?"

"We'll call him from the house after we talk to the family. With luck we'll be able to share the best news any of us have heard all summer."

****

# Chapter 52

Danny pounded on the door of the two-story Victorian style house that Melissa Harris and her family called home. Tessa had already rung the doorbell six times, with no response. It had taken the detectives nearly two hours to drive from the station to the Harris' upscale neighborhood on the outskirts of Fairbanks due to a deadly accident that was complicating the already heavy traffic brought on by residents leaving the city. Danny was already irritated before he and Tessa even walked onto the family's front porch. He had tried to call Melissa several times on the way over to the home but had not been surprised when her phone had gone directly to voicemail. But he hadn't expected to receive no answer when he'd called the Harris' landline. He was now totally out of any patience he had for the Harris family and whatever game they were playing by refusing to come to their door or answer their phone.

"Fairbanks police!" he yelled. "We need to speak with you now. Open the door!"

"You sure this is the right address?" Tessa asked as Danny's pounding was also met with silence.

"Yes it's the right address for Christ's sake. How dumb do you think I am?"

"Just asking."

"What the hell are they doing? Are these parents seriously hiding in their house?"

He pounded on the door again and shouted once more for the Harris family to please open their door.

"You're not going to get any answer there. You might want to stop pounding that door before you break your hand."

Danny and Tessa jumped simultaneously and turned to face a small elderly woman who had come up behind them on the Harris' front steps.

"Who are you?" Danny asked.

"I'm Marian Holmes and I live next door," the woman said, gesturing towards the neighboring house. "I couldn't help hear you yelling out here."

"What did you mean saying we don't get an answer?" Tessa asked.

"Seems obvious to me. The family isn't home."

"Do you know that for sure or are you just saying that because they're ignoring us?"

"I know it for sure. They left for Coldfoot about an hour ago."

Danny took an involuntary step back at the mention of Aleksei Nechayev's former home town and nearly fell into the Harris' front door.

"Coldfoot?" he asked, recovering his balance. "Why the hell did they go to Coldfoot?"

"Only place within driving distance where they could get a reservation. The hotel up there had a cancellation from an out of state tourist who doesn't want to come to Alaska now. Otherwise they wouldn't even have been able to get that."

"But why did they leave?" Tessa asked.

"Because of the fires. Everyone's leaving if they can."

Danny thought back to his conversation with Melissa. She had said "We all are!" when talking about Will and his family leaving the city but he hadn't questioned her on it. He'd been so focused on getting her to come in and give a statement he hadn't even paid attention to it. He'd certainly never imagined she meant her family was leaving this very afternoon.

"When did they make these reservations?" he asked the neighbor.

"I couldn't tell you. I just saw them packing up their car and they looked like they were in an awful hurry so I asked if they were okay. They assured me they were but they wanted to get out of Fairbanks." Marian shrugged. "I wasn't surprised. Like I said, everyone's leaving."

"What about you?" Tessa asked. "You're staying?"

"I'm too old to go running out of town. I'd just as soon stay in my own home and hope for the best."

Tessa reached out her hand and patted Marian's shoulder. "We're

191

all hoping for that. Thank you for your help."

"My pleasure."

Danny tried his best to smile at the neighbor as he followed Tessa down the porch steps and back to the waiting car. He couldn't manage it.

\*\*\*\*

# Chapter 53

"Can you even believe that?" Danny said as he fumbled in his pocket for his cigarettes.

Tessa glanced from the road to Danny. "Are you reaching for your cigarettes? Are you seriously thinking about smoking in my car?"

Danny scowled. "Please? Just this once?"

"Absolutely not."

"God dammit I need a cigarette after this day. That family just made those reservations today, I'd bet my ass on that. They're driving up to Coldfoot just to keep us away from their daughter."

"I imagine you're right but you're still not smoking in my car."

"They must have heard Melissa on the phone with me. Or maybe she freaked out herself and told them."

"Doesn't matter. They're gone."

"When they get their asses back to Fairbanks I'd like to charge them with obstruction."

Tessa laughed. "Sure. See how that goes over in the media. 'Police harass terrified parents desperate to protect their child...'"

"Maybe there won't even be a Fairbanks for them to return to though. At this point I can see that being the case."

"Don't say that. So this didn't work out. We'll find something else that does." Tessa drummed her fingers on the steering wheel. "What about Jennifer's cameraman?" she asked. "He heard the chanting too. Maybe he'll recognize Dzubenko's voice. We could talk to him unofficially. Just feel him out."

"If we ask him flat out if the voice is Dzubenko's and he agrees that will never hold up. They'll say we led him to the conclusion we wanted. Can you imagine how a lawyer for Dzubenko would go after us on that?"

"I said unofficially. If he does think the voice is Dzubenko's, maybe we can at least convince the Chief and the FBI agents to let us tail that son of a bitch."

"I like how you think, Tessa," Danny said. "I think I've been a good influence on you."

Tessa rolled her eyes. "Please. You think I didn't know how to be a cop before you came rolling into town? You know where Bob lives?"

Danny reached into his pocket again, this time procuring his phone. "No but I can find out. Let's head over there."

****

# Chapter 54

Robert Spencer had been placed on medical leave not long after witnessing the fire that had claimed Jennifer Higgins' life. He'd tried to continue working following the murder, but had been terrified to go out on an assignment with any of the reporters. The station owner had suggested therapy to help Spencer deal with the fallout from the trauma he had been part of and had granted the man's request to take time off.

Thus Danny and Tessa found him at home on the afternoon of August 21. Neither was surprised to see Spencer's haunted expression and hollow eyes as he opened the door and ushered them into his living room. They expected nothing less, having both seen more trauma victims than they could count.

"Mr. Spencer, thank you for meeting with us," Tessa said as she and Danny sat down next to each other on Robert's disheveled brown couch.

"It's not a problem," Spencer said, taking his place across from them on a worn matching loveseat. Spencer picked up the tv remote from an end table and turned off the movie he had been watching.

"You're a Godfather fan?" Danny asked, referencing the movie that had been playing.

"Who isn't?" Spencer replied.

"True enough." Danny dispensed with the small talk. "Listen, Mr. Spencer…"

"Please, just call me Bob."

"Great, Bob. We want to talk to you off the record for a moment. We're not asking you for any kind of statement and we know however you answer our question we won't be able to use the information officially."

"What's the point then?" Bob asked, clearly puzzled.

"It will help us," Tessa asked. "We just need you to be honest with us."

"Fair enough," Bob said, shrugging his shoulders.

"The day Jennifer was killed," Tessa continued, "You told us you heard chanting before the fire started. Do you remember that? Do you remember the chanting?"

"Of course I do. How could I forget it?"

"If you heard the same voice again do you think you'd recognize it?" Danny asked.

"I can't imagine I wouldn't."

"Have you seen any of the interviews with Jamie Dzubenko on the news?"

"That guy who says you're harassing him?"

"That's the one," Danny said.

Bob sat back on the loveseat and eyed both Danny and Tessa with growing suspicion. "What about him?"

"Do you think his voice could be the voice you heard chanting? Have you ever had the sense that his voice seemed familiar to you when you've watched him?"

Bob shook his head slowly. "I don't know…"

"Bob, we know how terribly difficult this must be," Tessa said. "I can't begin to imagine what you witnessed when Jennifer was murdered. But if you could just think about the chanting for a minute and remember the voice in your head."

"You think I've ever forgotten that voice? I don't need you telling me to remember it."

Danny held up his hand. "Of course you don't. We don't mean to upset you."

"Do you think if you listened to a recording of Mr. Dzubenko you'd be able to tell us if the voice sounds similar or not?" Tessa asked.

"I'm sure I could."

"Do you have a computer?" Danny asked.

Bob got up from the loveseat and walked into his dining room. He returned with an open laptop. "Of course I do," he said. "You're saying you want me to listen to one of those interviews?"

"If you don't mind."

Bob sat back down and opened his browser. He quickly brought up the Channel 10 website and clicked on one of the Dzubenko videos.

196

Within seconds, Dzubenko's voice filled the living room.

"I suppose I just couldn't keep quiet after I heard from my aunt that a police detective had traveled to Anchorage to harass her and bring back the terrible memories of the death of her brother. My father. What my family has gone through is horrible enough without having to deal with police harassment."

Danny watched as Bob listened to the man he was sure had killed Jennifer Higgins. He knew he shouldn't, but he found himself silently begging the cameraman to recognize the voice from the scene of the fire.

Bob's hands started to shake as he listened to more of the interview. While he stared at the screen, he no longer seemed to be seeing it. He suddenly slammed the laptop closed, silencing Jamie Dzubenko and making both Danny and Tessa jump in their seats.

"I don't know if this is the man who killed Jennifer," Bob said, shaking his head no as he spoke.

"You didn't recognize the voice?" Tessa asked.

"I don't know if I did or if I didn't. I can't say. It could be the voice I heard. But there's just as good a chance it isn't."

"Maybe if you listened again…"

"I don't think so," Bob said. "I can't help you. I'm sorry."

"Are you sure you can't just listen to a little more of the interview?" Danny asked.

"I told you folks I don't know! Christ, you're making me think this man is right about you railroading him."

"I'm sorry," Danny said. "I shouldn't have pushed it. It's just that you seemed so certain before that you remembered the voice."

"I thought I did. But all I can say now is it was a man's voice. I can hear the gibberish he was saying and I thought I could hear the voice too but listening to this I realize I just don't know anymore."

Tessa stood up from the couch. "We understand. And we are sorry, Mr. Spencer. Thank you for being honest with us."

Bob nodded and rose from the loveseat. "If you don't mind, I'll show you out. I don't want to talk any more about this."

"Of course."

Danny and Tessa remained silent until they were seated back in Tessa's car. "What do you think about that?" Danny asked. "You think he really couldn't recognize Dzubenko or he just freaked out and didn't want to think about it?"

"Hard to say. I almost felt like he went into a trance while listening to the interview. Did you see his hands shaking?"

"I did. And I think he did recognize Dzubenko's voice but just got too frightened to say so."

"Maybe. But either way this doesn't help us any."

"Let's talk to Jack about it. He needs to know that Melissa called me, and about what she said. Maybe he'll agree to at least let us keep an eye on Dzubenko."

"I doubt it. He's got the Chief all over his ass."

"I doubt it too but what have we got to lose?"

Tessa pulled out of Robert Spencer's driveway and headed back to the police station.

****

# Chapter 55

"What's going on?" Danny asked the desk sergeant Mark Chambers as he and Tessa returned to the police station. There was a palatable sense of energy and excitement in the air.

"The FBI agents found the arsonist," Chambers said. "They're heading over to pick him up now. He's been hiding out at some abandoned place on Chestnut."

Danny and Tessa glanced at each other and headed into the station to find Jack Meyer.

They didn't have to look far.

"Fitzpatrick! Tessa! I've been looking for you two. Was just getting ready to call you." Jack lumbered down the hallway towards the two detectives. "Where have you been?"

"We were out following up on a lead, Captain," Tessa said.

"Did Chambers tell you the news?"

"He did," Danny said. "Sir, can we talk to you in your office?"

"Of course."

Jack turned and headed back down the hall towards his always untidy office. He moved boxes of files from the two chairs in front of his desk.

"Have a seat," he said as he did so himself. "What's up?"

"Sir," Tessa said. "We have misgivings about the arrest the FBI agents are making right now."

"You do? Is this based on the lead you two were just following up on?"

"It is," she replied. "We talked to Robert Spencer, the cameraman for Jennifer Higgins."

"Christ that poor bastard," Jack said. "I've heard he's having a hell of a time of it."

"Yeah, he is," Danny said. "But we wanted to talk to him because he told us back when Jennifer was killed that he heard a man chanting before the fire started."

"And?"

"Do you remember the two kids who were in the woods at the baseball game and saw Nick Torrance right before he was killed?"

"Yes, I remember," Jack answered. "Where are you going with this, Fitzpatrick? Cut to the chase."

"One of the kids called me this morning and told me she had seen Jamie Dzubenko on the news and she recognized his voice. She thought it was the same voice that she and her friend heard chanting right before Nick Torrance caught on fire."

"Aw, Jesus. Really? You're still on Dzubenko?"

"Sir, we think there's good reason to be on Dzubenko," Tessa said.

"Can you bring this kid in and interview her?" Jack asked.

"No. She's afraid and doesn't even want her parents to know she called me. Tessa and I went over to their house to talk with them but the family left Fairbanks for the Arctic today. We can't get anything from the girl right now."

"So what does this have to do with Robert Spencer?"

"We thought he may recognize the chanting voice as Dzubenko's too."

"And did he?"

"No, he didn't. Or at least he said he didn't."

"What the hell does that mean?"

"Sir," Tessa said, "Danny and I both thought the man looked absolutely terrified while he was listening to Dzubenko's interview. It was like he went into a trance. His hands started to shake…" she paused. "We think he said he couldn't place the voice because he is so frightened. He is quite obviously still struggling to cope with what happened to Jennifer."

"But he specifically said he didn't recognize Dzubenko's voice?"

"He did."

"Then what the hell can we do with him?"

"Not much, we know," Tessa said. "But if we could just put more attention on Dzubenko…"

Jack glared across his desk. "Do you both want to get all three of us fired?"

"No, sir," Danny said. "We do want to save people from burning to death though."

"What did I ever do to deserve you and your self-righteous, smartass attitude, Fitzpatrick?"

Danny smiled. "You're a lucky man I guess."

Before Jack could respond, the meeting was interrupted by a bustle of activity at the front of the station. Danny and Tessa turned in their chairs to see the FBI special agents ushering in a tall and thickset man with his hands cuffed behind his back. Representatives from all the media outlets crowded the front door and main desk.

"You see that?" Jack said. "Lots of people think that guy right there is the one burning people to death around here."

"Yep, lots of people think that. I don't though," Danny said. "Neither does Tessa. And neither do you, sir."

"You're so sure of that, are you?"

"Yes, I am. Remember the guy on the video at Phillips' office? He was slight, thin..." Danny gestured towards the front door of the building. "That fool they just brought in looked big and burly to me. Not even close to the same body type as the man we watched burn Phillips to death."

"Alright, you know what?" Jack said. "You're right. You know damn well I think this FBI thing is bullshit, plain and simple. It's the Chief and the Mayor both trying to keep their jobs. Maybe this poor slob they just carted in here is an arsonist, but I think it's more likely he's just a perfect scapegoat."

"I guess we'll know in two days if the city starts burning," Tessa said.

"What exactly do you two think I can do? We don't have any evidence against Dzubenko and he's made monkeys out of all of us. And now that they've made this arrest and the media and politicians are going to start shouting it from the rooftops, I can't authorize surveillance on some jackass who isn't even officially a suspect. We're over a barrel here and you both know it."

Danny let out a breath. "God damn Dzubenko. Son of a bitch."

"I think at this point all we can do now is wait for the twenty-third. If the fires start, we'll know the FBI has the wrong guy and we can go after ours. Maybe we can catch the bastard in the act," Jack said.

Tessa and Danny looked at each other. Each nodded almost imperceptibly.

"Maybe we can," Tessa said.

\*\*\*\*

# Chapter 56

*August 22. 11:00 pm*

Tessa sat in her car three houses down from Jamie Dzubenko's apartment. She could see lights on on the first floor of the house, but no sign of anyone moving around. She hoped Dzubenko hadn't already left to start his sadistic festivities.

The lights of another car brightened Tessa's rear view mirror and she turned to see Danny's car coming slowly towards her, his headlights illuminating the darkness of the street. The sun had set about an hour ago and the clouds masked the twilight that normally kept the sky light. Tessa's thoughts had turned to winter and the coming dark days and she cursed the summer for going by so quickly. Even with this year's heat, she hated to see the end of the sun and the long hours of daylight.

Danny drove past her once, turned a corner past Dzubenko's house and eventually came back around to the street. He parked two cars behind Tessa on the opposite side of the street. Within seconds, her cell phone rang.

"Hi Danny," she said.

"Fancy meeting you here."

"It is quite a coincidence, isn't it?"

"What are you up to?"

"Just watching that house up the way. I heard there might be some trouble on this street."

"Yeah I heard the same thing. Maybe starting around midnight."

"Uh-huh."

"The AC in my car is acting up," Danny said. "Mind if I come join you in yours?"

"Not at all."

Danny left his car and walked quickly to Tessa's, crouching down in between other cars to keep out of sight in case Dzubenko happened to be looking out his window.

"You know I don't have the car running," Tessa said when he climbed into her passenger seat. "The AC isn't on."

"Oh, that's right. Well shit I'm here now, aren't I?"

Tessa chuckled. "If Jack finds out we're doing this, our asses are both toast I think."

"I think so too. But if we catch Dzubenko in the act I think we'll be forgiven. If not, I'll take the blame and tell them I forced you to help me."

Tessa raised an eyebrow. "And you think they're going to believe I let you force me? Please."

Danny laughed. "Alright, fine. I won't be a martyr. We'll both go down in flames."

"Fair enough." Tessa took a drink from a bottle of water she had sitting in the cup holder in between the two front seats. "I haven't seen any movement in the apartment. But the lights have been on since I got here."

Danny glanced out the window at the night sky. "Just when I was getting used to the sun, it's going to disappear on us again."

"Yep. September's right around the bend and before we know it the snow will follow."

Tessa stopped talking as a shadow crossed Dzubenko's window. "Did you see that?" she asked.

"I did."

"I wonder if he's getting ready to go out."

"I guess we'll find out soon enough. The 23rd is officially here in about 45 minutes." Danny opened the backpack he had carried to the car with him and took out a bottle of beer. He unscrewed the cap and took a long drink. "To Vulcanalia," he said, raising his beer and tapping it against Tessa's water bottle. "Here's hoping it marks the end of Jamie Dzubenko's reign of terror."

****

# Chapter 57

Jamie sat on his living room floor with his candles lit in a circle around him. He breathed deeply and slowly to calm his mind and prepare his body for the festival he was about to begin. He tried not to allow the nuisance of the police on his street to disrupt his concentration.

The arrest of the FBI's scapegoat arsonist had been such a gift that Jamie didn't bother to think that any cops may still be onto him. But he should have known those damn detectives would be continuing their harassment. He wondered if they really thought he was so inept he would not see them parked on his street. Had they forgotten he had the ability to make himself invisible to the human eye? One trip outside to his yard and he'd seen both of those idiots sitting in the woman's car and staring at his home.

If they wanted a show, he wouldn't disappoint them. The two of them reminded Jamie of dogs who won't leave a person alone even when the person makes it clear they don't like animals. They just couldn't mind their own business and stay out of Jamie's.

So now he'd give them what they wanted, a front row seat to his masterpiece. In fact, he'd even bring them in as audience participation.

He'd make sure they'd regret harassing him by making them his first victims of the feast. He hoped their last thoughts would be how sorry they were to have ever crossed paths with Jamie. The thought of that made him smile.

The two nosy busybody cops would regret the day they first darkened his door when he set them on fire and watched as they both burned to death.

**\*\*\*\***

# Chapter 58
*August 23. 2013 12:00 am*

"Do you smell that?" Tessa asked.

"What?"

"Smoke. And I don't mean from your damn cigarettes."

Danny sniffed the air. "You're right. Something's burning."

Tessa pointed towards a row of flames in Dzubenko's backyard. "It's the grass in Dzubenko's yard!"

Danny stared at the small fire and felt his heart constrict in his chest. "He's starting."

They sat frozen, unsure what action to take. A siren flying by the cross street behind them made both detectives jump.

"That was a fire engine," Tessa said.

The police radio crackled to life and the two detectives listened to the report of a fire in an abandoned building on River Street.

"His work," Danny said. "I'm sure of it."

As the fire in Dzubenko's yard started to spread, Dzubenko himself emerged from his house. He stood next to the flames and stared directly at Danny and Tessa.

"He knows we're here," Tessa said. "He's been watching us."

Before either could get out of the car, Dzubenko disappeared into the smoke.

"Jesus Christ," Danny said. "Let's get over there."

They each took their guns from their holsters and ran to Dzubenko's house. Tessa pointed towards the far end. "I'll take this side," she called.

Danny nodded and ran around the back to the steadily growing fire. He saw Tessa on the other side of the yard, with Dzubenko coming up behind her.

"Tessa! Behind you!" he yelled.

Danny saw Dzubenko grab Tessa around the neck before she could turn and stop him. He started to run towards her just as the fire erupted and turned into a wall of flame separating him from the other half of Dzubenko's yard.

"Tessa!" Danny screamed.

He ran around to the front of the house and towards the side where Tessa had dropped out of sight just seconds earlier. He saw nothing but the inferno Dzubenko's yard had become. Over the roar of the flames, Danny heard chanting. The chanting Melissa and Bob had heard, he was sure of it.

"Dzubenko? You son of a bitch!"

The chanting grew faint as Danny ran to the front of the house and frantically looked through the windows, desperate for a sign of his partner. The house was empty, save for a circle of candles and an ancient book opened to what must have been Dzubenko's spells.

He ran back to the yard, calling for Tessa again and again. As he reached the yard, the fire died out as quickly as it had begun. Nothing remained but a few dying embers. Danny ran through the smoldering grass to the spot where he had seen Dzubenko first grab Tessa. He found nothing there but her gun.

As he grabbed his phone to call Jack and ask for help, it rang, startling him and causing him to nearly drop it. He felt a gush of relief as he saw the caller ID.

"Tessa?" he answered. "You're okay?"

"She's okay for now," Jamie said. "That won't be the case for much longer though."

"God damn you. Where are you? Where have you taken her?"

"I'm in my car right now and your partner is with me. I parked a few blocks over yesterday just in case some idiots like you were outside my house when I was ready to begin the festival."

"You're in your car? You know I can trace that right? You dumbass."

"You could have traced it, yes. Except that I stole someone else's car in order to prepare for my event. If you look you'll see my own car is parked right in front of my place. In fact you're probably standing next to it right now. A blue Honda?"

"Fuck you. I can run traces on all the stolen cars then. I'll find you."

"I'm actually hoping you will find me. So much so that I'm giving you a little hint."

"What is it?"

"I'm taking your partner to where it all began for me. I can't think of a better way to celebrate Vulcanalia."

Jamie ended the call before Danny could respond.

Danny stood in the street, wanting to throw his phone on the ground and smash it to bits but knowing that wouldn't solve anything except taking away his ability to communicate with Dzubenko and, by extension, Tessa. He walked quickly back to his car, forcing himself not to look at Tessa's car and the bottle of beer that he had just set in her cup holder minutes earlier. He didn't even notice the increase of sirens, their noises now reverberating across the city.

Sliding into his car, he called Jack before turning on the ignition.

"Fitzpatrick?"

"Yes. I need help, Jack. Or more accurately, Tessa needs help."

"What? What the hell happened? What are you two doing?"

"We were staking out Dzubenko."

"What? Jesus Christ!"

"We were right about him. Now he's got Tessa and he's going to kill her if we can't find her first."

"How do you know this? What happened?"

Danny quickly explained the fire, Tessa's disappearance, and the call made from her phone. "Dzubenko's driving a stolen car," he said. "We need to go through all the cars stolen in the last few days. Or maybe in the whole goddamn month. Who knows when he stole it?"

"I'll get every officer available on it. We've also got fires going off all over the city. I wonder if he's bringing her to one of those."

"Where are they?"

"All over! All abandoned buildings so far. The first one was called in a little after midnight. Since then we've had five more calls. From what I've heard from the fire department they all seem to have started burning at the same time."

"I don't think he's taking her to one of them," Danny said. "The hint he gave was that he was taking her where he started."

"Griffin Park?" Jack said. "Where he killed Fugate?"

"Maybe. I'll head over there. Can you send back-up?"

"On it."

Danny hung up without further conversation.

****

# Chapter 59

As Danny drove towards Griffin Park, he knew he was headed in the wrong direction. It was a good guess, but it was wrong. The park wasn't what Jamie meant when he said he was going where it all started.

Danny kept driving the same way as he tried to think of another place Jamie could be headed. Where had it all started for him?

Danny swerved to the side of the road to avoid a fire truck that came speeding up behind him and was steadily blowing its horn at the few drivers on the road. He watched as the truck careened off ahead of him, hoping that it was headed towards another empty building and not a person or a house.

A house. Danny tapped his fingers on his steering wheel and thought back to his meeting with Frank Wainscott. He had been so certain that Jamie Dzubenko had burned down his family's house. Had that been where it all started for him?

Danny quickly brought up the case file from the documents on his phone and looked up the Dzubenko address. He recognized the street name, as it was now the focus of a debate over what to do with the land. The houses had been razed as part of an economic development plan prior to the start of the recession in 2008. The company had gone bottom up in the recession and the development had been stalled for years. It was now nothing more than an abandoned street with half-built retail and office buildings that would never be finished.

That was where Dzubenko had Tessa, Danny was sure of it. He would be there now, waiting for Danny to show up. He grabbed his phone to call Jack as he turned the car around and tore off in the opposite direction, ignoring the blare of horns and speeding through a red light. Danny had no intention of making Dzubenko wait long.

\*\*\*\*

# Chapter 60

Danny pulled into the abandoned industrial development that had once been the street where Jamie Dzubenko lived as a child and instantly felt removed from the sirens, screams, and flames that were terrorizing the rest of Fairbanks. There was nothing and no one here but Dzubenko, Tessa and himself.

A half-built parking garage stood to the left of the development entrance next to a pottery store sign with merely the shell of a building attached to it. Across the drive, a planned bookstore and café were no more than foundation and two disconnected walls. Danny had no idea where the Dzubenko house had been in this now razed neighborhood, but he knew it wouldn't be that hard to find him, wherever he was holding Tessa. There was nowhere for him to hide here.

Dzubenko had no intention of hiding, as Danny quickly discovered when the man stepped out in front of his car. He dragged Tessa beside him, his arm locked around her neck. Danny swallowed his rage and stopped driving. He stepped out, his gun in his hand before he got out of the car.

"That gun isn't going to do you any good Detective Fitzpatrick," Dzubenko said.

"I beg to differ on that."

Danny sniffed the air, smelling the unmistakable stench of burned flesh. He glanced at Tessa and noticed a smoking patch of burned skin on her arm. Her face was contorted with both pain and terror.

"You piece of shit," Danny said.

"You mean because of Detective Washington's arm? I just needed to keep her in line until you got here. I wanted to get you both together. The two of you have been such a thorn in my side. But back to your gun, I'm not afraid of it. I'm not one of your usual dirtbag suspects. I'm above all that. Would Vulcan be afraid of a gun?"

"Listen jackass, the only Vulcan I know anything about is Mr. Spock so your dramatic monologue is wasted on me. Let Tessa go before I show you just what my gun and I can do to you."

As he talked, Danny remembered the amulet Madeline Locklear had given him. He kept his gun on Dzubenko as he fished in his pocket and found it. He threw it to Tessa and was amazed when she managed to catch it in spite of Dzubenko's grip around her neck. Fear and pain clearly hadn't slowed her reflexes.

"Hang on to that, Tessa," Danny yelled. He felt a sliver of hope that the amulet may actually be worth something when he saw it start to brighten in Tessa's hand.

Jamie glanced down at the now glowing amulet. His lip curled in disgust. "Is that from that quack Locklear?"

"I'm thinking she might not be such a quack," Danny answered.

"Are you really foolish enough to think a touchy-feely moron like that can stop me? You think she has a single clue about my kind of magic?"

Danny shrugged. "No harm in trying."

"You're wrong about that. But your partner's the one who is going to feel the harm."

"What?" Tessa said, the first sound she had made since Danny arrived.

Before she could say another word, Jamie muttered something unintelligible and the amulet's glow became a pulsating red. Within an instant, it turned to fire in Tessa's hand. She screamed and dropped the amulet, which burned out and shriveled into dust at her feet.

"Still think Locklear might be able to stop me?"

Danny released the safety on his gun and pointed it straight at Dzubenko's head. "I knew it was a longshot," he said. "I'm not though. And I'm done playing games with you now, asshole. Let Tessa go and step away from her."

"I don't think so."

"It's not gonna take much for me to blow your head off your neck, Dzubenko. Let her go goddammit!"

Danny could feel his forehead beading with sweat and his heart begin to beat erratically in his chest. His hands shook as he pointed the gun. Thoughts of the last time he had aimed a gun at another human being flooded his mind.

"Fuck this," he said aloud. "You won't screw it up this time."

"Screw what up?" Dzubenko asked.

"Nothing. I was talking to myself. And now I'm giving you one more chance. Let my partner go before I shoot you down like a goddamn dog."

Instead of responding, Dzubenko began chanting. His eyes rolled back in his head as he spoke.

"YA zaklykayu BEELZEBUTH~, LUCIFER~," he said. "MADILON…"

"What are you saying?" Danny yelled. "Shut up and let her go, Dzubenko!"

"SOLYMO~, SAROY ~, Vizyt!"

Flames erupted on Tessa's already burned arm. And Aleksei Nechayev's smug laughter echoed between Danny's ears.

"Oh my God, no! Please, no! Danny!" Tessa screamed

"Stop chanting, Dzubenko! Shut up and stop chanting!" Danny's hands trembled, ruining his aim on Dzubenko. "I don't want to hit you, Tessa. I can't get a good shot. Goddamit, let her go!"

"Pozhezha!" Jamie yelled, completely ignoring Danny's commands. "Spalyuvaty!"

Tessa's leg caught fire as the flames on her arms jumped to her chest. Her screams turned to unintelligible cries of anguish.

"Spalyuvaty!"

"Shut the fuck up!!" Danny screamed.

Danny fired the gun and hit Dzubenko in the arm. He immediately stopped chanting, his trance-like state shattering along with his humerus. He let go of Tessa and looked at Danny in amazement.

"You shot me."

Tessa fell to the ground, rolling frantically to extinguish the flames.

Danny fired the gun again, this time hitting Dzubenko in the chest and causing him to fall to his knees.

As Dzubenko opened his mouth to speak, Danny fired again. His shot hit Dzubenko's heart, silencing him for good. Danny stepped closer and fired again. Dzubenko's blood splattered onto his face and clothing.

He heard the sound of approaching sirens and knew Jack and the other police officers had arrived on the scene. He stood over Dzubenko's dead body and kept firing until his magazine was empty.

\*\*\*\*

# Chapter 61

Danny dropped his gun and fell to the ground next to Tessa.

"You alright?" he asked.

Tessa remained silent. She started to shake as if freezing cold.

"Jack and the others are here now," Danny said. "We'll get you to the hospital. You'll be alright." He put his arm around her shoulders, careful not to touch her burns, which still smoldered as the skin bubbled and burned. In spite of the burns, Tessa's skin felt clammy and cold.

"We're even now, yeah?" Danny said, desperate to talk in the hopes of keeping Tessa from going into shock. "You found me in the Arctic and now I found you here."

Danny rocked Tessa as Jack came running up to the scene.

"Mother of God. What happened?"

"This asshole set Tessa on fire. She's badly burned and she's gone into shock. We need to get her to the hospital, now."

Jack quickly called for paramedics and returned his attention to the scene in front of him. He pointed at Dzubenko's body. "You shot him?"

"I did. He wouldn't stop his goddamn chanting. He started the fire with that and was going to burn Tessa alive just like he did to those other people."

"Chanting. What the hell? How did he set her on fire?"

"Chanting! Didn't I just say that? It's some kind of magic. I don't know how he did it."

Jack walked to Dzubekno's lifeless body and glanced at Danny's emptied gun on the ground next to it.

"How many times did you shoot him?"

"I shot him until he shut up."

"Was he armed?"

"He was armed with his mouth. And his fire, however he did it."
Danny scowled. "Don't start with me, Jack. He started to kill Tessa,
period. Once she's been seen by a doctor she'll be able to tell you
herself."

Jack held up his hands. "Alright, alright. She's gonna be alright
though, isn't she?"

"She's got bad burns, I know that much. Look at her for Christ's
sake. Her skin is still bubbling."

"Jesus Christ Almighty."

Danny heard the sound of the approaching ambulance, but
realized the cacophony of sirens that had reverberated throughout the
city earlier that night had stopped.

"Are the other fires still burning?" he asked.

"No, I don't think so. I talked to the Fire Chief when we were on
our way over here. He said the fires were stopping."

"They stopped when this fucker died," Danny said, pointing to
Dzubenko.

The forensic investigators and coroner arrived at the scene and
cordoned off the area around Dzubenko.

"They really don't need to do a big investigation," Danny said.
"I'm telling you straight out I shot him. There's no mystery here."

"You know we need to cover all the bases," Jack said.

As the ambulance arrived for Tessa, Danny gently lay her on the
ground and stood up, making way for the paramedics.

"You need to be seen yourself?" Jack asked.

"At the hospital? No. I'm fine."

"You don't look it."

"I'm fine."

He squeezed Tessa's clammy hand before the paramedics moved
her into the ambulance.

"I'll follow you to the hospital, Tessa," he said. "But first I'll go
check on Maya for you."

"We're going to need to talk about all of this, Fitzpatrick," Jack
said. "You know that as well as I do."

"We'll talk about it."

Danny turned his back on Jack and the rest of the officers and
investigators who now swarmed the scene. He walked to his car and

Julie Flanders

drove out of the development, anxious for a drink and a cigarette.

# Chapter 62
*August 23, 2013 12:00 pm*

Danny walked into the police station having not slept in more than 24 hours. He'd at least showered though, so he assumed his colleagues would be able to stand being in the same building with him. He wasn't sure if he could stand being with himself though. Not even the hottest and longest shower had been able to rid him of the stench of burning flesh, blood and gunpowder.

"Are you okay, Detective Fitzpatrick?" Mark Chambers asked. "I heard you weren't hurt."

"Yeah, I'm fine, thanks."

"I stopped at the hospital to check on Detective Washington before I came in this morning but they wouldn't let me see her. She was still in ICU."

"She's burned bad but she'll be okay," Danny said.

"Thank God. The fire department is still on guard all over the city but so far it seems the fires stopped during the night."

"Right. Because we stopped the guy who was setting them."

"The FBI agents say they're still looking for someone who may have been working with their arsonist. They think he may have had an accomplice who started the fires last night."

"They're idiots," Danny said.

With that, he'd had enough small talk. He headed towards his desk but kept going past it, walking instead to Jack Meyer's office. His boss sat at his desk, unshaven and hollow-eyed. Danny clearly wasn't the only person who hadn't slept in far too long.

"I have a feeling you want to see me, Captain."

Jack looked up at Danny and nodded. "Close the door and have a seat, Fitzpatrick."

Danny complied and stared across his captain's desk, thinking back to the day he had dropped his badge and gun on a different captain's desk and walked away from the Chicago police department. He had thought then that he was done with being a cop. He should have stuck with that.

"Tessa's alert now and has given a statement that Dzubenko set her on fire and you saved her life. She corroborated everything you've said about what happened last night. Including the fact that Dzubenko set a fire at his own home to separate the two of you and trap her."

"Imagine that. I was telling the truth. And yet I hear that our FBI friends are still obsessing over their arsonist."

"They're trying to save face. The fact is the asshole they've got is an arsonist and has caused a lot of trouble around the state. He's a freak. A pyromaniac or whatever the hell you call them. So it's no loss that he's gone down."

"Right. But he had nothing to do with Dzubenko's killing spree. So why are they looking for an accomplice of his that could have set the fires last night?"

"Because no one can figure out how Dzubenko set any of the goddamn fires. Including the one he set to burn Tessa. Tessa herself says she doesn't understand how he did it. People want answers and we don't have them."

"There's never going to be a satisfactory answer. Just like there's never been a satisfactory answer to the question of how Aleksei Nechayev managed to disappear into the Arctic in the middle of winter without even a pair of snowshoes. I've found, sir, that there are things in this world that simply don't make sense."

"Well that's not going to cut it. Christ people were burned alive here. And the whole goddamn city could have burned down."

"And Jamie Dzubenko did all of it. People will forget about it soon enough and stop asking questions about it as long as they know the killer has been stopped and no one is going to be running around setting them on fire any time soon. The conspiracy theorists will eat it up but no one will ever truly be able to figure it out."

"Again, Fitzpatrick, that's not going to cut it. We've got a big problem here."

"What's that?"

"You emptied your revolver into an unarmed man. You fired at least three shots after the one that killed him. You were found at the scene covered in his blood. This same unarmed man happened to be all over the news as a victim of police harassment. That's our problem."

"Unarmed? You ask Tessa how 'unarmed' he was. I'd call setting someone on fire being armed. He was threatening me with the same fate. The only reason I was able to stop him was because he was so damn delusional he thought a gun wouldn't hurt him."

"But how was he setting the fire? Don't you see, that's what's causing this mess! Did he have a cigarette lighter he was touching to Tessa's skin? A match? She says he had nothing. All she will say is he was chanting."

"Right. He was chanting. Just like he was chanting before he killed Nick Torrance and Jennifer Higgins. And you can bet if we'd had sound on the surveillance video at the church we would have heard it before he killed Richard Phillips as well. That was his weapon, sir. It's some kind of fucking magic. Illusion. He's the murderous version of Harry Houdini. Call it whatever you want so that people will believe it. That's what it was. Magic"

Elbows on his desk, Jack put his head in his hands and slowly rubbed his eyes. "I actually believe you. But I don't know how we're going to sell a story like that."

"Sell? Where are we working? Advertising?"

Jack let out a breath and looked across his desk at Danny. "The Chief has ordered an investigation into all of this. And he believes that the department made a mistake promoting you and letting you continue to work without any mental health treatment after what happened to you up in the Arctic. He thinks you were already a vulnerable man after the murder of your wife and that near-death experience was too much for you to handle."

"Are you kidding me? So the pyromaniac isn't going to be the scapegoat in all this, is he? I am."

"Danny…"

"No, screw this. I never should have come to work at this god-forsaken place."

"The Chief wants you placed on administrative leave. You're to receive a mental health evaluation and counseling, and a psychiatrist will need to determine when you're fit to return to duty."

Danny met Jack's eyes. "You agree with all this?"

"No, I don't. But I do think you need help. I've thought that since we found you in the Arctic. And why wouldn't you? Christ look at what you've been through in the past few years! This is an opportunity to take some time and heal, Fitzpatrick."

"Fuck healing. And fuck this department. I'm not going to any psychiatrist or counselor or anyone else."

"It's your choice. But you're on paid leave as of today. I need your badge and gun."

Danny stood up and defiantly lay both on the desk, his eyes never leaving Jack as he did so. "I did this once before, you know? Voluntarily, that time. When I did I swore I was never going to work as a cop again. I should have stuck with that."

He turned and walked out of the captain's office without another word. He stopped at his desk and grabbed what few personal items he kept here at the station then headed for his car, ignoring Mark Chambers as he walked out of the building. Danny drove away from the Fairbanks police station without looking back.

\*\*\*\*

# Chapter 63

"What are you going to do?" Tessa asked from her hospital bed.

"I have no idea. Maybe I'll work as a PI. Maybe I could be like Magnum."

Tessa laughed and immediately grimaced at the resulting pain. "Don't make me laugh," she said.

"I'm sorry. What about you? Any idea when you'll get out of here?"

"I don't know. They're going to have to do skin grafts on my arm and leg. And my lungs were damaged from the smoke."

"Well, I picked Maya up last night and she's staying with Sox and me. She's not happy but she'll live. You don't have to worry about her. She's got a home with us for as long as you need."

"I'm glad. Thanks for taking care of her."

"Hey, it's not like I have anything else to do, right?" Danny glanced around the sterile hospital room. "You and I have spent more than enough time in hospitals in the past year, haven't we? Christ I was only in here a few hours and I couldn't stand it."

"Danny," Tessa said. "How did Dzubenko start the fires?"

"You said it yourself. Illusion, remember? He was the world's greatest magician."

"It wasn't illusion." Tessa gently lifted her bandaged arm from the bed. "This isn't illusion. It's a real burn. From a real fire."

Danny looked away and stared at the wall. He let out a breath and turned back to his partner. "Tessa, remember when I tried to tell you up at Nechayev's place that he was a monster? A real monster? You thought I was just in shock and talking nonsense. I wasn't."

"What are you saying?"

"I'm saying I've learned in the past year that things I always thought were nothing more than horror stories and fairy tales were not.

They're real. Dzubenko started the fires with magic. Witchcraft. He came from a long line of witches, going back centuries in the Ukraine."

"Witchcraft," Tessa said. "Witches?"

"Right. I know it sounds crazy. I know you probably think I'm crazy..."

"No, I don't. I would have before Dzubenko set my arm on fire with his voice but now..." Tessa shook her head. "Maybe I'm crazy."

"I thought I was crazy too, if it makes you feel any better. I still think I am."

"Well, we all think you are," Tessa said, a sly grin pulling at the corners of her mouth.

"Right. I'm the crazy cop who needs a psychiatrist, I forgot. Glad I can amuse you."

"We'll be crazy together, Danny."

****

# Chapter 64
*August 30, 2013*

The yellow caution tape still surrounded the former home of Jamie Dzubenko, but Danny knew the police were long done with the scene. They had found little evidence linking Dzubenko to the fires, which had done nothing to help Danny's case that his shooting of Dzubenko had been entirely justified. But he wasn't surprised at that, as the police had no idea what to look for in terms of evidence. And if Tessa's testimony and very real burns weren't enough to absolve Danny, nothing would be. He didn't care either way. He had no interest in rejoining the force even if they were able to prove Dzubenko had been the sole arsonist who had nearly turned Fairbanks into an inferno.

He knew he should stay away from the home, but his curiosity got the better of him. He hadn't been able to stop thinking of the book Frank Wainscott had seen Dzubenko holding as his home burned down. The book Constance Davenport had said was the spell book owned by her grandfather, the man who had tried to kill Aleksei Nechayev with the same magic his great-grandson had used for such destruction and terror. Danny had seen an old book on Dzubenko's floor when he'd peered into the man's window before Tessa had been captured. He knew the book he wanted was in the home and he wanted to see it for himself. And, he wanted to destroy it so its magic could never be used to harm anyone else.

The door was unlocked, as Danny knew it would be. Dzubenko's upstairs neighbor had briefly returned on the twenty-fourth to pack up his belongings and move out for good. The house was vacant.

But not empty, as Danny discovered when he opened the door and walked inside.

"Hello, Detective Fitzpatrick. What a surprise to see you here."

Danny stared wide-eyed at the figure of Aleksei Nechayev in front of him. He was sitting at Dzubenko's kitchen table dressed in black jeans and a black button down shirt with the sleeves rolled up to his elbows. A tea kettle and cup sat on the table in front of him. Fear overtook Danny and he stood rooted to the floor, frozen and unable to speak.

Aleksei set down his tea and crossed his arms in front of him. He leaned back in his chair, looking at Danny with a puzzled expression. "You don't need to be afraid of me. How many times must I tell you I don't wish you dead?"

"How did you get in this house?" Danny croaked. "And what the hell are you doing here?"

"Which do you want me to answer first? Never mind, I'll go in order. I got into the house because your erstwhile adversary Jamie Dzubenko is dead. I can't enter a living person's home without an invitation, but once that person is dead I'm home free. And as for what I'm doing here, it's simple. I came for Jamie Dzubenko's book. And now I'm waiting for the sun to set so I can leave here and be on my way."

Aleksei picked up his tea and took a long drink. "I certainly didn't expect company, but I'm glad to see you all the same. I've read what a mess you're in."

"I'm not in a mess."

"You're not? You're an unstable cop who emptied a weapon into an unarmed man and now you've been let go until you prove yourself mentally fit to return to the job. I'd call that a mess."

"I don't want to return to the job."

"Really? That's a shame. You're good at it. I hate admitting that but you caught me so I have to believe you're better than the average idiot who flashes a badge." Aleksei gestured to the chair across the table from him. "Why don't you join me? Have some tea? We can catch up."

Danny shook his head. "I told you if I ever saw you in this state again I'd kill you."

"Right. But how do you plan on doing that? Do you have a wooden stake with you this time?"

"No but I've got a cigarette lighter." Danny looked outside at the rays of the setting sun peering through the curtains. "Or I could push you out into the sun. It hasn't set yet."

Aleksei laughed. "I'd like to see you try that. You really think you can push me? And as for the lighter, go ahead and give that a shot. I'll rip your heart out of your chest before your thumb even touches the roller."

"Why do you want the book?" Danny asked. "I came here to destroy it."

"Not a bad idea, but I'd rather keep it myself."

"Why?" Danny asked again.

"Because a man almost killed me with this book. If I hadn't managed to outsmart him I would have been killed before my life as a vampire even had a chance to begin. I don't want this heinous book to ever fall into the wrong hands again."

"So why not just let me destroy it?"

Aleksei shrugged. "Who's to say I might not find a use for it myself at some point?"

"I thought you said only those born into witchcraft could do these spells?"

"I did. And that's true. But maybe I'll meet a witch someday who wants to join up with me. Can you imagine what we could accomplish? We'd give a whole new meaning to the idea of a power couple."

"I'm not going to let you do that," Danny said, hesitantly taking a step towards Aleksei. "I'm destroying that book."

Aleksei chuckled. "I admire your persistence. But I'll say it one more time. You can't stop me." He fixed a penetrating gaze on Danny. "You can't beat me."

"I can try. I don't have a damn thing to lose."

Aleksei finished his tea and stood up from the table. "I see the sun is nearly set and I can get out of here. I'm leaving Fairbanks."

Danny blocked Aleksei's path. "You'll have to get through me first."

Aleksei sighed as if dealing with a petulant child. "Have it your way. As I've told you many, many times, I have no desire to harm you. But since you've forced my hand, I will."

Aleksei moved behind Danny with the speed of a cheetah and gripped Danny's neck in his arms. "This feels like déjà vu, doesn't it? We've been here before as I recall."

Danny struggled to break free as Aleksei tightened his grip and blocked the air from Danny's windpipe. Spots decorated Danny's line of vision before the room went black and he found himself enveloped in darkness.

When he awoke, Aleksei was gone. But this time, Danny wasn't tied up. He got shakily to his feet and noticed a note on the table next to Aleksei's empty teacup.

"I hope I've finally convinced you now that I have no interest in killing you. I doubt our paths will cross again as I also have no interest in returning to your hellish state. I've wanted to visit Scandinavia for a long time, and I'm looking forward to returning to a land of the polar night now that autumn is nearly upon us. In spite of your continued hostility towards me I once again wish you well, Detective. And you're welcome for my help in stopping Jamie Dzubenko."

Aleksei had left the note unsigned. Danny picked it up and shoved the paper in his pocket. His neck ached and his throat felt raw, but otherwise he had come through his third meeting with the vampire unscathed.

He rubbed his neck and searched for the reason he had come to Jamie Dzubenko's home in the first place. But he knew it was a useless search. The book of magic was gone.

Danny could only hope that there were no witches in Scandinavia.